EXTREME VINYL CAFE

ALSO BY
STUART McLEAN

FICTION

Stories from the Vinyl Cafe

Home from the Vinyl Cafe

Vinyl Cafe Unplugged

Vinyl Cafe Diaries

Dave Cooks the Turkey

Secrets from the Vinyl Cafe

NON-FICTION

The Morningside World of Stuart McLean

Welcome Home: Travels in Smalltown Canada

EDITED BY STUART McLEAN

When We Were Young:
An Anthology of Canadian Stories

STUART McLEAN

EXTREME VINYL CAFE

[signature]

VIKING
CANADA

VIKING CANADA

Published by the Penguin Group

Penguin Group (Canada), 90 Eglinton Avenue East, Suite 700,
Toronto, Ontario, Canada M4P 2Y3 (a division of Pearson Canada Inc.)

Penguin Group (USA) Inc., 375 Hudson Street, New York, New York 10014, U.S.A.
Penguin Books Ltd, 80 Strand, London WC2R 0RL, England
Penguin Ireland, 25 St Stephen's Green, Dublin 2, Ireland (a division of Penguin Books Ltd)
Penguin Group (Australia), 250 Camberwell Road, Camberwell, Victoria 3124, Australia
(a division of Pearson Australia Group Pty Ltd)
Penguin Books India Pvt Ltd, 11 Community Centre, Panchsheel Park,
New Delhi – 110 017, India
Penguin Group (NZ), 67 Apollo Drive, Rosedale, North Shore 0632, New Zealand
(a division of Pearson New Zealand Ltd)
Penguin Books (South Africa) (Pty) Ltd, 24 Sturdee Avenue, Rosebank,
Johannesburg 2196, South Africa

Penguin Books Ltd, Registered Offices: 80 Strand, London WC2R 0RL, England

First published 2009

1 2 3 4 5 6 7 8 9 10   (RRD)

Manufactured in the U.S.A.

LIBRARY AND ARCHIVES CANADA CATALOGUING IN PUBLICATION

McLean, Stuart, 1948–
Extreme vinyl cafe / Stuart McLean.

ISBN 978-0-670-06447-2

I. Title.

PS8575.L448E94 2009   C813'.54   C2009-903831-5

Visit *The Vinyl Cafe* website at **www.vinylcafe.com**

Visit the Penguin Group (Canada) website at **www.penguin.ca**

Special and corporate bulk purchase rates available; please see
www.penguin.ca/corporatesales or call 1-800-810-3104, ext. 477 or 474

To Jess Milton,
friend and producer,
verba desunt

My favourite pastime? To laugh!

Tenzin Gyatso
14th Dalai Lama of Tibet

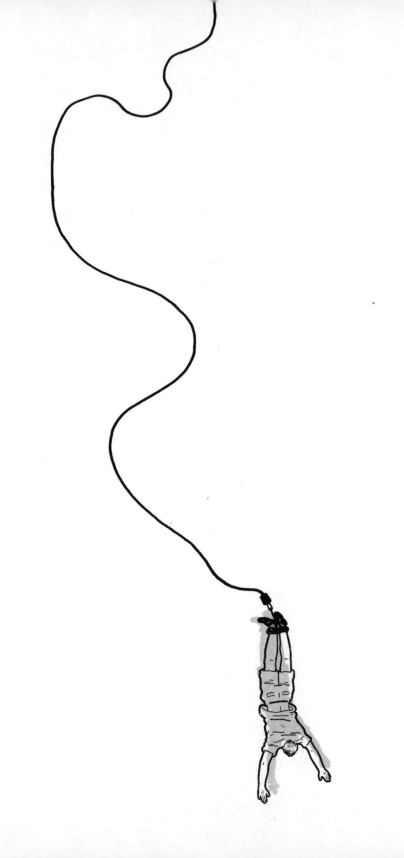

CONTENTS

INTRODUCTION

Now before we begin, I thought I should say a word or two about the title. I imagine that many of you picked this book up because you were taken by the striking cover design and intrigued by the title. You were probably thinking to yourself, *Hmm*, Extreme Vinyl Cafe. *That sounds interesting. I wonder what Extreme Vinyl Cafe means.*

I want to be upfront about this. I have no idea whatsoever.

Many months before this book was due to hit the shelves, I was called into my publisher's office and told that they had a great new concept for me. In the conversation that followed, I have to admit, I was a little overwhelmed—by the marketing terms, by the sales strategy and by the very comfy chairs. To be honest, I think I drifted off for a while. But before I lost consciousness, I vaguely remember mention of extreme sports, and supercharged energy drinks, and, possibly, high-definition television. And then the next thing I remember, I was being ushered out the door, with handshakes and backslapping and general words of congratulation. I realized that I must have agreed to something, and that "something" appears to be the title of this book.

Several weeks later, still confused, I asked the marketing manager to explain the concept to me again. "Oh you know,

Stuart," he said. "*Extreme*. Like we're taking fiction to a whole new level."

A whole new *level*. That begged an obvious question. What level were my stories at before? And where was I supposed to be taking them now? The only thing I could figure out was that maybe I was meant to provide something extra for my readers with this collection. Something new, and beneficial, and helpful. But what?

So I rounded up the people who work with me on *The Vinyl Cafe* radio show and asked them. "With my stories," I said, "what could I improve, what could I add? What else could I do for my readers?"

"For starters," said my long-suffering story editor, Meg Masters, "you could learn how to spell."

"But that would only help *you*," I pointed out.

"You could charge them less," said production assistant Louise Curtis. "Books are quite expensive, you know."

"But that's up to the publisher," I said.

"How about this?" said my producer, Jess Milton. She reached into a file cabinet, pulled out a folder and slapped it down in front of me. "Why not answer some of your mail?"

Now it may surprise some of you to know that since I started *The Vinyl Cafe* radio show and have been telling my stories in concert, people have begun to see me as somewhat of an authority. An authority on what exactly has yet to become clear, but let's just say they've been coming to me with questions, looking for my wisdom and guidance. And even when I don't immediately know what to say, or how to help them, their questions do linger in my mind and sometimes creep into my writing. In some cases, I feel that a story I have already written might be of some assistance to them. At other times, it is as if the question has tickled my imagination, and, quite unconsciously, I begin to answer it as I tell my tales.

Here, then, are fifteen stories that could serve as answers to fifteen intriguing questions that you might share with the people who originally presented them. I hope that in reading the questions, and then the corresponding stories, you find this book to be a "miracle cure," and "a bargain at twice the price," or at the very least, you find yourself at a whole new *level*. Whatever that means.

EXTREME VINYL CAFE

Dear Stuart,

I seem to have developed a nasty rash. (I am enclosing four photos for your perusal.) I took these shots at the photo booth at the train station, so you have to look carefully. But look at the second one, which is just of my legs (I had to stand on the stool to take it). I know those marks look like freckles, but that is because these pictures are in black and white and the exposure is weird. But if you could see them in colour, you would know they don't look like freckles at all unless freckles are red and sort of weepy. Ignore the last shot—that is the security guard's arm and not mine and that is why there are no rashes on it.

Do you think I should see a doctor?

Your friend,
Miles

Dear Miles,

Yes.

SAM GOES GREEN

The first Dave heard of it was back in the fall.

He heard from his friend Dennis, who was in town working on a Patsy Cline project. Some guy was recording an album of Patsy Cline covers—note-for-note instrumentals, no vocals. The fellow had hired Dennis to play bass. They were working nights to save money, which meant Dennis had the afternoons to kill. He started dropping in to the Vinyl Cafe.

By the end of the week, Dennis, who has an eye for a deal, and not a lot of restraint once he has spotted one, had bought a Sun recording by Johnny Cash called *The Songs That Made Him Famous*, and a Best of Otis Redding, and the Red Beatles, and Marvin Gaye's *What's Going On*, and *The Many Moods of Charlie Louvin*.

On Friday he was working his way through the cheap bin at the back of the store—*Vinyl's Last Stop*—when he whooped, making Dave look up from behind the counter. Dennis was holding an album in the air and swaying back and forth. "Merle Haggard's breakthrough record," said Dennis.

"That shouldn't have been in there," said Dave when Dennis brought it to the cash. He didn't *really* mind. It was nice having Dennis around.

And that's when Dave heard. That Friday, from Dennis.

"Jake's going out again," said Dennis. "He's rounding everyone up."

"You're kidding," said Dave.

"He called last night," said Dennis. "Wanted your number."

Jake James was the front man for Jake and the Apostles. Dave had met him the afternoon the Apostles opened for Jefferson Airplane.

"I thought he was going to be the next big thing," said Dave.

"Everyone did," said Dennis.

It turned out Jake had stage fright. It turned out every time Jake got a break, something would happen. He would get sick. Or blow his voice.

Or not show up. Get the time wrong. Something to mess it up.

"He's going to call," said Dennis. "He said you promised."

It took a week, maybe two. Jake didn't call; he dropped by the store. When he walked in, Dave held his hands up in the air. He didn't make Jake ask. Jake walked through the front door, and Dave held up his hands and said, "I'm in."

"It's just a week," said Jake. "You could bring Morley."

And that's why Stephanie came home for spring break. Dave was road managing Jake James's week-long comeback attempt, Morley was along for support, selling product and keeping things even, and Stephanie came home to look after Sam.

"He's not old enough to stay alone," said Dave. "We'll pay you."

Stephanie didn't have plans anyway. It worked out well for everyone.

The night before they left, Dave and Morley finished Sam's room. They had been working on it for a couple of weeks, upgrading it from a *little* boy's room. There was a new bed, a new desk, a new rug. The final step was new paint— Moonraker, a shade of yellow between Springtime and Lantern Light.

The yellow paint was making Morley blue.

"You don't understand," she said one night. She had a red bandana covering her hair, a paintbrush in one hand and a tiny piece of blue plastic in the other. "You don't understand," she said again, holding out the plastic piece. "All *this* is over. Forever."

"I don't even know what that is," said Dave.

Morley sighed and dropped the little piece of plastic into a set of rolling plastic drawers. "It's a tail stabilizer for a Sigma 6 Dragonhawk."

The night before they left, Morley took Sam out to buy sheets for his new bed. He chose flannel Ninja Turtle sheets. Morley was beaming when she got home. "Just when you have given up hope," she said.

"Did he buy them in earnest or irony?" asked Dave.

"Don't want to know," said Morley.

Morley and Dave left on Friday morning.

"We'll be back next Sunday," said Dave. "We'll call every night. Six o'clock."

"Fun, fun, fun," said Sam under his breath as he and his sister watched their parents pull out of the driveway. Given their past experiences under similar circumstances, this was a stunning flash of optimism.

When Stephanie was thirteen and babysitting her little brother for the first time, she had made Sam, who was about seven at the time, spend the entire afternoon cleaning her bedroom. At sixteen, she'd invited someone over—Sam never knew who—and he had been sent to his room with a video, a family-sized bag of chips and strict instructions not to come out for the entire evening.

Something about their relationship had changed. It was nothing either of them had done. It was just the relentless tides of breakfasts and dinners, of socks and underwear; time tumbling them the way the ocean tumbles glass—smoothing the sharp edges, rolling the hard green of impatience into the emerald softness of love. It was just the work of the ocean and the laws of the family asserting themselves.

Since she has been away at school, Stephanie's appetite for bugging her brother has ... dissolved.

"We'll go out for dinner," she said. "There's a place I want to show you."

It was the way she said "we" that Sam noticed.

"I'm going to meet Becky," she said. "She needs to buy a dress. I'll call you later. We can meet."

There, thought Sam. *She did it again.*

Then Stephanie gave Sam her cellphone number, but nothing else. No instructions or even advice.

He liked this. This was cool. He felt grown-up and independent. They should have sent Stephanie to university years ago.

Sam spent that Saturday morning amusing himself, *and* annoying Arthur, the dog, with his Nerf gun. Peter Moore came over in the afternoon with his new video game. Murphy came over too. They played for six hours.

Dave phoned at six. "The boys can stay for dinner. You could order pizza," he said.

Then he added, "The healthiest choice is the one with the grilled vegetables and no cheese."

"We'll get that one, for sure," said Sam, rolling his eyes. "Can we have it with steamed broccoli?"

After Peter and Murphy left, Sam stayed up watching DVDs. Stephanie didn't seem to care when he went to bed. Or whether he took a bath. Or what he ate. He stayed up past midnight on Saturday. Later on Sunday.

On Monday, at the end of library class, Mrs. Atkinson asked Sam to stay behind.

"Are you feeling okay?" she said.

"What?" asked Sam. Sam happened to be feeling on top of the world.

"You don't look well," said Mrs. Atkinson. "I thought I would ask."

Sam shook her off. He felt fine. As he bounced down the hall he was thinking, Mrs. Atkinson is *weird*.

Then it happened again. After lunch. In between periods four and five, Mr. O'Neill stopped him in the hall and asked him the same thing.

"Are you feeling okay? You look a little sallow."

"I'm fine," said Sam. He didn't say anything about Mrs. Atkinson. But it was strange. Twice in a day. It made him wonder.

He went to the boys' room and peered at himself in the

mirror. He looked fine. But after school, they were playing ball hockey in Peter's driveway, and Peter said, "What's the matter with you?"

And Sam said, "What do you mean?"

Peter said, "You look green."

Sam asked Stephanie that night.

"Do I look okay?"

"Your jeans are too baggy," said Stephanie. "You should get a job and get decent jeans. When I was your age, I was buying my own jeans."

"Jeans are *supposed* to be baggy," said Sam, looking at his legs dubiously.

"Not like *that*," said Steph.

When his parents called, Sam wanted to tell them what Mrs. Atkinson had said about him looking bad. But he didn't want to worry them—especially his father, who had a tendency to overreact.

"Before you go to bed," said his father, "check the oven and make sure it is off. Also the back door. Make sure the back door is locked. And don't light any candles. You're not lighting candles, are you?"

"No," said Sam. "I'm not lighting candles."

"What about your sister?"

The next morning they had gym first period: basketball. Skins versus Shirts. Sam was a Skin. After five minutes Mr. Reynolds pulled him onto the sidelines. "You look a little green," said Mr. Reynolds. "You'd better sit out."

Sam went into the boys' room and looked in the mirror again. It wasn't just his face. It was his whole chest. He spun around and peered over his shoulder at his back. He felt a rush of anxiety. Something *was* wrong. It was like he had a tan, but weird. He changed mirrors, and it was the same. It was his ears and his cheeks too. It was like he had a bruise all over his body. But different. Brighter. Sort of greeny grey. Maybe he *wasn't* feeling so good.

When gym was over he tried to brush it off.

"It's just the colour of my skin," he said. "You shouldn't judge someone by the colour of their skin." The truth was he was feeling worried.

When Sam's parents phoned at supper, Dave said, "Before we left, I meant to check the smoke alarm and I forgot. Will you check the smoke alarm? There should be a little light flashing every ten seconds. If it's not flashing every ten seconds, call us on Mommy's cell."

"I'm fine," said Sam.

Obviously he wasn't fine.

"You *do* look a little green," said Stephanie later that night. "Do you feel okay?"

The truth was he didn't feel okay. The truth was he was feeling tired. The truth was he was getting a headache.

"I have a headache," he said.

"Take off your shirt," Stephanie said. Sam stood in front of her with his shirt off.

"Turn around."

She said this quietly, ominously. Then she said, "You should go to bed."

"I'm fine," said Sam. But he didn't sound convinced. He headed for his room. Stephanie came upstairs ten minutes later. "People turn orange from eating too many carrots," she said.

Sam was lying in bed, on his back, the covers up to his chin. "I'm not turning orange," he said. "I'm turning *green*."

Stephanie said, "Because maybe you've eaten too much green stuff."

"But I haven't had a single vegetable since Mom and Dad left," said Sam.

Stephanie was back ten minutes later with a plate. There were beets, an apple and a cut-up red pepper.

Sam said, "You want to turn me red?"

Stephanie said, "Red and green are complementary colours. I am trying to balance you."

"I feel sick," said Sam.

The next morning he was definitely worse. He came downstairs and there was an undeniable mouldy pallor to his skin. It seemed worst around his head, his wrists and his neck, but his whole complexion was vaguely off.

"I am going to phone Dr. Keen," said Stephanie. "You should stay in bed."

Stephanie's concern scared him. She *never* paid him *this* much attention. And she wasn't just paying attention—she was being kind and concerned. It could only mean one thing: He was dying.

"I'm okay," he said.

Sam went upstairs. He didn't want to stay in bed. He wanted to get dressed. He opened a drawer and stared at it. He pulled out a green sweatshirt. Maybe if his shirt was green, it would mask his skin. He stared at himself in the mirror. He couldn't decide whether it made it better or worse.

He came downstairs and stood in front of his sister.

"Do I look like a broccoli?" he asked.

Stephanie said, "You have an appointment with Dr. Keen this afternoon. You should stay home from school."

He went back upstairs and got back in his pyjamas. He read for a while, but he was feeling worse and worse. It was hot under the covers. He began to sweat. He rubbed the perspiration off his forehead onto his pyjama sleeve. And he froze.

There was a bright green smear on his shirt sleeve. His sweat was the colour of lime Kool-Aid. Now his *sweat* had turned green. That could only mean one thing: Whatever he had was coming from inside of him.

It was suddenly obvious to him. He had been colonized by some weird green thing. A space creature, possibly. Or some sort of pond algae. Maybe his insides were going mouldy— like swamp water, or a piece of cheese that had been in the fridge too long. It really didn't matter what it was, because it was pretty obvious that whatever had taken hold of him wanted out. His chest could erupt at any moment.

Murphy came over after school.

Sam said, "I think I have an alien."

Murphy nodded earnestly. Then he took off his glasses, pulled out his shirt and polished his glasses on his shirttail, which is what Murphy does when he is thinking very hard. He polished his glasses, then he put them back on and bent over Sam, who was lying on his bed despondently. Murphy peered at Sam, coming closer and closer until their faces were less than six inches apart. Sam was getting uncomfortable.

Sam turned his head and said, "What are you doing?"

Murphy reached out and took Sam's chin and twisted it so they were face to face again, and he said, "Breathe."

"Why?" said Sam.

Murphy said, "I want one too."

At five o'clock, Stephanie took Sam to Dr. Keen.

On the way there, Sam was thinking Dr. Keen would tell them there was nothing to worry about. Sam thought Dr. Keen would say that boys his age turned green all the time, that it was a perfectly normal thing and would go away in a couple of days.

But that's not what happened. Dr. Keen took one look at Sam and frowned. He agreed that Sam did not look at all well. Dr. Keen listened to Sam's heart, and looked in Sam's ears. He took Sam's temperature. Then he shook his head and said he was flummoxed.

"We'll do some tests," said Dr. Keen.

Sam said, "Do you think maybe I have an alien?"

Dr. Keen said, "I don't know what you have. I'm a little perplexed."

Dr. Keen was writing in his file. Sam wasn't sure if he was talking to him or talking to himself. He was muttering. This is what he was saying: "If he were blue, that would be a different matter. If he were blue, then cyanosis or something else that involves his heart and lungs ... if he were *yellow*, well then ... primary biliary cirrhosis, Wilson's disease, yellow fever, liver or pancreatic cancer, jaundice, hyperbilirubinemia, anemia, hepatitis A, B, C, D, E, or Y, or, of course, gallstones."

"Hyperbili ... what?" said Sam nervously.

Dr. Keen looked up at him and said, "What? Oh. Hyperbiliru-binemia. But you're not yellow." He looked back at the file and muttered, "And you're not blue, either."

"No," said Sam. "I'm green."

"I'm going to take some blood," said Dr. Keen.

Sam looked away as Dr. Keen got ready to draw the blood.

"Deep breath," said Dr. Keen.

Then he said, "All finished."

Sam said, "Well?

Dr. Keen said, "Well what?"

Sam said, "What colour is it?"

On the way home, Dr. Keen's list of diseases echoed in Sam's ears. He couldn't remember all their names ... just hyper-bilirubinemia, and that there were a lot more. Blue ones and yellow ones.

When he got home, he crawled morosely back into bed. Pretty soon he was crying. He wanted his mother and father. Why were they away when he needed them? Probably he would be dead when they came home.

Maybe he should call them. If his mother were here, she would sit beside him on the bed and tell him not to worry. If his father were here, he would ... panic.

Okay, he wasn't going to phone them.

He got out of bed and began to pace. Maybe he could figure this out. Stephanie was right. If carrots made you orange, it made sense that green stuff made you green. He had to avoid anything green.

He went over to his desk and started making a list: beans, broccoli, Brussels sprouts. There was a lot of green stuff when you thought about it: lettuce, spinach, peas—though it had never occurred to him just how much—asparagus, apples.... He kept adding to his list. No wonder he was turning green. Cabbage, kiwi, and cucumbers ... he was slowing down. He stared at the paper for a moment without writing anything. Then he added *Collard greens. Bok choy. Mint-chocolate-chip ice cream.*

He was staring at his list when Murphy called.

Sam said, "The doctor did a blood test."

Murphy said, "What colour was it?"

Sam told him about Dr. Keen's list.

Murphy said, "I'd better come over."

Murphy was standing at the foot of the bed wiping his glasses.

Murphy said, "It's worse than we thought. All those blue and yellow diseases."

Sam said, "I don't have them."

Murphy was shaking his head. "When you mix blue and yellow together, what do you get?"

Sam shrugged.

"You get green," said Murphy. "It is possible you have all of them."

It was the worst night of Sam's life. A sense of doom settled upon him. His mother and father called, but he couldn't remember what they talked about.

Murphy was right; the doctor wouldn't have taken blood if he didn't think something horrible was happening. In his head, he had already got the tests results back. He had hyper-bilirubinemia. His life was as good as over.

At nine o'clock the phone rang. He prayed it was his mother. He and Stephanie had decided not to tell their parents anything until they got the test results. They didn't want to ruin their trip. But if it was his mother, he was going to tell her now.

It wasn't his mother, of course. And the wheels of the night ground on. Sam lay in bed working through all the possibilities. What if it wasn't fatal? What if it was worse than that? Exactly *how* green could he turn *without* dying? What if he was as green as a frog by the time he got to high school? And what about university, when he didn't know anyone? Would they hold it against him if he was green?

Maybe they wouldn't even let him into university, even if his marks were good enough. What would happen at the interview when they saw he was as green as a broccoli? They had done a unit on the civil rights movement in school. He knew you weren't allowed to discriminate against people because of the colour of their skin—white, brown, black or yellow. But the books never mentioned green.

And even if he got into university, would he ever get a job? Or a girlfriend? What girl would want to take him home to meet her parents if he was green?

He fell into a fitful sleep around midnight. But he didn't sleep well. He kept waking up.

Murphy phoned in the morning, all excited.

"You don't have to worry. It's okay. You're not the only one. I just heard that the prime minister is going green. And he wants other people to turn green too."

Sam said, "Did they say how you do it? Is it a voluntary thing?"

He clung to that for an hour. Maybe *he* was one of the first. Maybe he would go down in history as a trailblazer. Maybe in two hundred years he would be a folk hero. Like Jackie Robinson. Maybe he would be the first green boy to go to university. The first green Olympian. Like that.

Or maybe it wasn't that at all. Maybe his hormones were messed up. Maybe he would keep getting greener the older he got. Or worse. Maybe this was just the beginning. Maybe as he got older, his skin would keep changing colour. First green, then blue, then ... oh this would be bad ... what if he turned purple? It was bad enough being green, but purple would be pure torture. Or what if he was both? What would life be like if you were multicoloured?

He fell asleep at noon wishing that he could just worry about pimples like a normal kid.

Dr. Keen called in the afternoon and said the test results were normal. But *he* wasn't. He was still green.

"I am not sure what to think," said Dr. Keen. "If it continues for a few more days, you should come back in."

"Can I go to school?" Sam asked.

"I think so," said Dr. Keen.

It was obvious Dr. Keen didn't have a clue what was going on.

But Sam was certain about one thing. When his mom and dad called at supper, he was going to tell them. His mother, that is.

It was his father who called.

Sam said, "Can I speak to Mom?"

Dave said, "Mom is right here. There are just a couple of things I want to go over first."

"I want to speak to Mom," said Sam.

"Tonight is garbage night," said Dave. "I want you to empty the garbage cans in the upstairs and downstairs bathroom and take everything out *before* you go to bed. And make sure the lid is on tight so nothing can get in.

"Also, make sure the milk is still good. If it's off, Stephanie should buy some new stuff tomorrow."

Sam said, "Please can I speak to Mom?"

Dave said, "One more thing. If you want to use your new sheets, make sure you wash them first."

"Pardon?" said Sam.

"The Ninja Turtle sheets," said Dave. "Make sure you wash them before you use them. 'Cause if you don't ..."

Sam interrupted his father. He was talking on the portable phone. He was sitting in his bed. He was beginning to feel a wave of relief descend on him. "If I don't wash them first ..." said Sam. He was looking down at the Ninja Turtle on his pillow, at the *green* Ninja Turtles on his sheets. "If I don't wash them ... I'll turn green, right?"

"Right," said Dave. "Now do you want to speak to Mom? She's right here."

"Naw," said Sam, "it's okay. I'll talk to her tomorrow."

Sam had already hung up.

He jumped out of bed. He grabbed his robe on his way out of his room. He was heading for the bathroom. He was heading for the bathtub, about to have the first bath he had ever really wanted in his life.

Dear Stuart,

Last Sunday night we went over to my mother's house for dinner and, as usual, before the night was done, she brought up the time someone demolished her entire stash of homemade jerky. This was like twenty years ago.

She used to keep the jerky in a tin on the counter in plain view and I was only sixteen at the time and starving, so I don't think I am to blame.

But I feel guilty and wonder if it is time to fess up. Everyone I ask tells me that I should totally tell, but they don't know my mother, or at least they don't know her when it comes to jerky. Anyway I know you used to date her when you were at camp, and I thought you might have an idea.

Sincerely,
Elizabeth Watson

Dear Elizabeth,

How nice to hear from you. I remember your mother well, or rather, I've had some trouble forgetting. I had an unfortunate incident with her jerky too. If I were you, I wouldn't approach her. Not in person, anyway. If you really feel strongly, I would suggest you have a third party there. People can be very prickly about food. I have attached a cautionary tale you might find interesting.

THE BIRTHDAY CAKE

They say love is blind. We all know they're right. And there is no end to the mischief a myopic heart can hatch, no end at all. But you don't have to be lovestruck to stir up trouble. Those lesser emotions can be just as dangerous.

No one would ever say Bert Turlington loves Dave. But Bert wouldn't deny that he feels a certain fondness, he might even say affection, for his neighbour. It is not love—more the accumulation of feelings that bind people together when they live side by side for many years, the small kindnesses and courtesies of their "arranged marriage."

So you could forgive Bert his neighbourly heart when he blurted out his invitation to Dave that night in the park.

You might. But Bert's wife, Mary, didn't.

"You what!?" said Mary.

Bert had invited Dave and Morley to drive with them to Montreal for Harold Buskirk's sixty-fifth birthday.

"And to stay with us?" added Mary. "In Rene's house?"

"It just came out," said Bert. "Unexpectedly."

Dave had said something about how he and Morley weren't sure if they were going to make it to the party. They hadn't made hotel reservations and … you know.

And Bert thought….

"No," said Mary. "Don't use that word. You *didn't* think. There wasn't any *thought* involved."

Harold Buskirk, who used to live up by the park, was turning sixty-five. Pretty much the whole neighbourhood was going to Montreal for the party. People had been working on sketches and speeches and songs.

Mary had been working on the cake. And not just any cake. For Harold, she was creating a masterpiece—a Frangelico-soaked chocolate fudge cake with white chocolate fondant and an orange buttercream and truffle ganache filling. It was Harold's retirement as well as his birthday. Mary was going to decorate her cake so it looked like a golf course—complete with little buttercream golf balls and a marzipan foursome standing triumphantly on the ninth tee.

Bert and Mary were driving to Montreal. They were staying at Rene Gallivan's house. Rene Gallivan is Mary's boss. Rene was in Florida, or Palm Springs. One of those places.

"You said it was a mansion," said Bert. "I thought there would be plenty of room." There was that word again. Bert was talking to himself. Mary had stormed off.

They left on Saturday morning, just after breakfast. Not that anyone actually *ate* breakfast. They were supposed to leave before breakfast and take a break on the road for brunch, but Mary had a moment with the fondant, and amid the last-minute cake flurry, brunch was lost.

There they were, on the road, two in the afternoon and only halfway to Kingston, two hours behind schedule. The four of them were in Bert's Volvo, their luggage in the trunk, Dave and Morley in the backseat and Mary in a state.

The cooler, with the cake, was wedged onto the armrest between Dave and Morley. They could barely see each other.

As they roared past Kingston, Dave said, "There's a great burger joint up ahead. If anyone felt like—"

"No stopping," snapped Mary. "There's no time for stopping."

At Iroquois, Dave, who was completely famished, made a lame joke that if he could have his cake *now*, he wouldn't *eat* any at the party. Mary whirled around and said if Dave as much as breathed on her cake, he could start walking.

There is no doubt Mary was wound up. The cake was iced with the fondant, but she still had to add the decorations, and it had to chill after that. And Mary had told Harold they would be at the club early, to help with the set-up.

They were two and a half hours behind schedule when they pulled up in front of Rene Gallivan's limestone house on Upper Walnut Crescent, a little-known cul-de-sac near the top of Westmount Mountain.

"Holy crow," said Dave as he unfolded himself from the backseat.

He was staring at the huge red oak doors, at the mahogany fluting around the lintel and the maple rosettes on the door's frame, at the lead-paned windows, at the thick stone walls.

"My," said Mary. They were all standing on the sidewalk staring now.

"Wow," said Bert.

"Oh dear," said Morley.

"Remember everyone," said Mary. "We have to leave every-thing *exactly* the way we found it."

She was staring at Dave.

"Oh dear," said Morley, again.

As Dave stepped through the threshold and into the marble foyer, Morley put her arm on his elbow and whispered, *"Don't-touch-anything."*

The kitchen turned out to be in the basement. It was the kind of a kitchen where help, rather than family, worked.

It had a fireplace.

"Holy crow," said Dave. "You could roast an ox in there."

It also had a walk-in cooler.

"Look at this," said Dave.

Mary was decorating her cake, sticking little marzipan flags carefully into the centre of the little greens. Morley was standing beside her, holding a bowl of brown icing for the sand traps. Bert was wiping down the counters.

Everyone was tiptoeing around—trying not to disturb a thing, trying not to make a mess. And no one was trying harder than Dave.

"I'll take the luggage to the bedrooms," said Dave.

Soon enough the cake was decorated and in the fridge, and everyone was ready to go. The cake, however, was not. The cake had to chill for at least an hour, or better, two. "As long as possible," said Mary.

But Mary was already supposed to be at the party.

Dave said, "You guys should go."

Dave said, "I'll stay here. I'll bring the cake when it's ready."

Someone had to.

Morley wrote down the address of the banquet hall so Dave could take a taxi. Beneath the address she wrote: *Please don't touch anything.* Then Morley and Bert and Mary left in Bert's car. Once they were gone, Dave set off to see if he could find something to eat.

On any other day he might have slid down the majestically curving banister from the second floor to the foyer. Or gone for a dip in the indoor saltwater pool. He might have had a steam or toured the wine cellar. But this wasn't any other day. He peeked in the wine cellar and stuck a finger in the pool. He touched one of the decanters of whisky and then fetched a towel and rubbed off his fingerprints. Dave was trying his best. Really.

The house had everything. Everything, that is, except a morsel of food. It was while he was looking for anything even remotely edible that Dave found the most amazing feature of the mansion: a wood-panelled elevator. It was the kind you might see in an old British hotel, about the size of a phone booth.

He opened what he thought was a cupboard door and there it was. It had brass fittings and a brass needle over the door to show which floor you were on.

He would have taken a ride, but he didn't have time to waste. They were waiting for him at the hall.

He went downstairs and fetched the cake from the cooler. It was rather touching: the icing golf course, with the greens and flags, the marzipan golfers and the little buttercream shrubs all around the edge. He carried it carefully over to the counter.

He wasn't going to mess this up.

Okay. He had everything. Wait a minute. No he didn't. The

address for the party was upstairs in his bedroom. He started up the stairs. Then he stopped dead. He shouldn't leave the cake unattended. The house was so vast; there might be dogs or cats or any number of things wandering around that could get into it. He fetched the cake and started up again. Four floors. Wait a minute—the elevator. He should take the elevator. The elevator would be safer.

He went in backwards. The brass door accordioned behind him. It was like stepping back in time. To a dimmer time—just before electricity.

He stood there, in the dimness, the cake safely beside him on the floor. He grabbed the elevator handle and plunged it to the right. Nothing happened.

He brought the handle back to the centre, opened the door and shut it and tried again. This time there was a bang, and a shudder, and a sudden lurch. Then the elevator started to move. He could almost feel the chains hauling him up, as if there were two or three men at the top of this elevator, and not strong men either, huffing and puffing as they turned some rusty crank.

"Come on," said Dave.

The elevator was moving in small, jerky increments. The shaft seemed to be too loose for the car. There was a lot of wobble.

And then there was no wobble at all. There was nothing. Absolutely nothing.

"Are we moving?" said Dave.

They weren't moving—they being Dave and the cake. Not up, that is. But that didn't mean there was no movement—there was still plenty of movement. The little car felt as if it were swinging back and forth, like a bucket on the end of a rope.

"Hello," he called.

"Hello," he called again. "Anybody? I am trapped in the elevator."

There was no reply.

"Help," he called. "I am in the elevator."

He hit the walls with his hands. Bang. Bang. Bang. Bang. He sat on the floor. He stood up. He took a deep breath and reached out and put his hand on the door handle. He opened the elevator door.

He was staring at a wall of plaster lathing. There was a big 3 written on the lathing in red chalk. He felt a wave of claustrophobia. He felt as if he had been buried alive.

"Help," he called, again.

He sat in the corner, with his head in his arms. He realized he might die in here. But really, what did that matter? If he didn't get the cake to the hall on time, Mary would kill him anyway.

An hour went by. The party would be just beginning. Dave was still in the elevator. And he was still hungry. He was wondering whether, when you were starving to death, if you gnawed off and ate your own arm that would count as sustenance. Or if eating your own arm would be a zero-sum game.

Jean-Claude Van Damme wouldn't eat off his arm. Jean-Claude Van Damme would haul himself out the emergency door in the ceiling and climb up the cable to safety. Dave glanced up at the ceiling. There was no emergency door. He felt a wave of relief. He would rather die in there than climb up a cable to safety.

He stared at the cake.

Surely Mary wouldn't miss one of those little buttercream shrubs.

Mary, had, actually, only just missed Dave.

"Shouldn't he be here by now?" said Mary to Bert. The guests were beginning to arrive. The party was getting going.

"He'll be here," said Bert, with more hope than conviction. "He is probably sitting in a taxi right now, with the cake in his lap."

Morley, who was standing just within earshot, helped herself to a glass of wine. A large one.

Bert was half right. Dave was *not* in a taxi. But he did have the cake in his lap. He had eaten every second shrub.

Half an hour later the little golf course had shrunk from nine to seven holes, the marzipan foursome was a twosome and Dave was eyeing their little golf cart. And that was when he spotted the emergency phone. It didn't fill him with hope. There was no dial. It was covered in dust. He picked it up and brought it to his ear.

The headquarters of ProCor Security Inc. is not what you would expect if all you knew of them was their shiny web page. Their web page features pictures of high-rises, and fit men in well-fitting uniforms, and a dog leaping over a fence, and a con-trol panel that looks like the command centre for a space flight.

The headquarters of ProCor Security is actually in the middle of a shabby industrial part of town, in a tiny cinderblock building with a flat roof and a peeling wooden sign. It looks more like the office of an auto repair shop than the headquarters of a security firm.

On Saturday evening, when Dave picked up the emergency phone, ProCor Security, the other end of that phone, and therefore Dave's only salvation, was in the hands of a university student. The student, a part-time employee, was beginning his second-ever overnight shift. And he was stretched across three office chairs in front of the surveillance panel, so deeply asleep that he wasn't only snoring, he was drooling. The hands that were holding Dave's life were tucked under his head.

The student had been trained the previous night by the woman who had the shift before him. She had been in a hurry to leave. His training lasted less than fifteen minutes. She showed him the computer and said nothing about phones.

So when a phone began to ring, it took the student by complete surprise. He sat up with a jerk and looked around. He was so dopey with sleep he couldn't figure out where the ringing was coming from.

When he finally opened the cupboard on the far side of the room, he almost fell over. There wasn't a phone in there. There were fifty phones in there—all of them attached to the wall, all of them red, all of them missing their dials. They looked like the kind of phones you might use to launch a missile strike. Except for the dust. They were all covered in dust.

There were so many of them it was impossible to tell which one was ringing. The student started picking the phones up at random. Before he found the right one, the ringing stopped. It took him awhile to get back to sleep after that.

About an hour passed before the phone rang again. This time he ran to the cupboard right away. This time he got the right phone on the fifth ring.

"Hello?" he said.

The student was as surprised as Dave to find someone on the other end of the line.

"Who are you?" the student asked.

"I am stuck in an elevator," said Dave. Then just to be sure this person on the phone understood the severity of his situation, he added, "with Mary's cake."

"Where?" said the student.

"In the elevator," said Dave. "I'm all alone in here."

"Which elevator?" said the student.

"How many elevators are there?" said Dave.

"I don't know," said the student. "I'm new."

Dave explained about the house on the mountain and the cake and the party.

"I know where I am going," said Dave. "But I don't where I am."

The student said, "Is this like a test or something?"

An awful thought came over Dave. He wasn't talking to a security guard in Montreal. He was talking to a call centre in Mumbai.

Dave said, "Are you in Mumbai?"

The student said, "Are *you* in Mumbai?"

Dave said, "I'm in Montreal. You've got to get me out of this elevator."

The student said, "This is just my second shift. I've never done this before. I can't roll trucks if I don't know where you are. We get fined. Call me back when you know where you are." And he hung up.

Dave stood in his elevator staring at the handset in disbelief. He was so hungry he could barely think straight.

Desperate times require desperate measures.

He slid the cake so it was half off the tray and held it very carefully over his head. Then he reached up from the bottom and stuck his hand right into it. He pulled out a fistful of the truffle ganache filling.

Mary would never know.

He sat on the floor licking the icing off his fingers.

He picked up the phone again.

It rang ten times.

"Hello?"

"It's me," said Dave.

"Me too," said the student.

"Listen, I'm sorry I hung up," said the student. "I am a little scared."

"Me too," said Dave. "What are *you* scared of?"

"I'm scared I might get fired if you die. Do you think I would have to put it on my resumé?"

It took them half an hour to figure it out. There was a number on the phone: 52. They were talking on phone 52. All the other phones had different numbers. The student found a binder with a legend, and in it an address that corresponded to each phone number.

"You are on Upper Walnut Crescent," he said.

Back at the hotel, Mary was beside herself. The main course had been served and there was still no sign of Dave.

Bert said, "I'll go. I'm sure everything is fine."

But he wasn't really sure.

Morley, now on her third glass of wine, was feigning interest in a conversation with a man just big enough to shield her entirely from Mary Turlington's sight.

Mary stared at Bert. Mary said, "You stay here."

When Mary's taxi pulled up in front of the Gallivans' house, the fire trucks had been there for about fifteen minutes. So Mary missed the part where they drove the axe through the red-oak front doors. But she was there when the elevator started to make whirring sounds and then began to drop smoothly. She was there when the brass doors opened onto the glass-strewn foyer. And she was there to see Dave, huddled over her cake like a raccoon huddled over a garbage can, his hands and face covered in icing.

He had been trying to smooth out the cake surface with his fingers. He held out the cake and smiled at her like a child handing in a class project.

"Safe and sound," he said.

They both stared at the cake without saying a word, and as they did the lone marzipan golfer, standing by what was now the sixth and final hole, started to sink slowly—first to his knees and then to his waist, as the entire cake began to collapse into itself as if it were built on a giant sinkhole.

Neither of them said anything for most of the long drive back to the party. At Dave's suggestion, they stopped at an all-night grocery store and bought a replacement cake, the only cake left in the store. A My Little Pony cake.

The drive home the next day was even quieter—perhaps "steamier" captures it better—as was the rest of the autumn. It was the first time there was a noticeable strain between the neighbours. It was not actual unpleasantness, just a determined quiet, which was unpleasant enough in itself. And then one night, out of the blue, Bert called and invited Dave and Morley for dinner. They couldn't have picked a worse night. It was Dave's birthday. Dave and Morley had reservations at a little Italian place they favour.

"Cancel them," said Morley.

And so Dave and Morley went next door, and dinner was not unbearable, though it was awkward. Mary was obviously trying to let bygones be bygones, but you could tell it was a struggle. And then it was time for dessert.

And out came a birthday cake.

A My Little Pony birthday cake.

Mary carried it to the table and set it down. Then she blew out the candles, picked up the cake and very carefully turned it over. She scooped a handful from the bottom of the cake and plopped it on Dave's plate.

She said, "That's the way you like it, right?"

Dave sat there, staring at his plate, not knowing what he should do, looking back and forth at Mary and his wife. It was

Morley who started to giggle. Morley giggled. Mary smiled. And then Bert started laughing so hard he was pounding the table. They all laughed and laughed.

It was really their only choice. You swallow your pride and you laugh, or you fight. So they laughed. It's what good neighbours do.

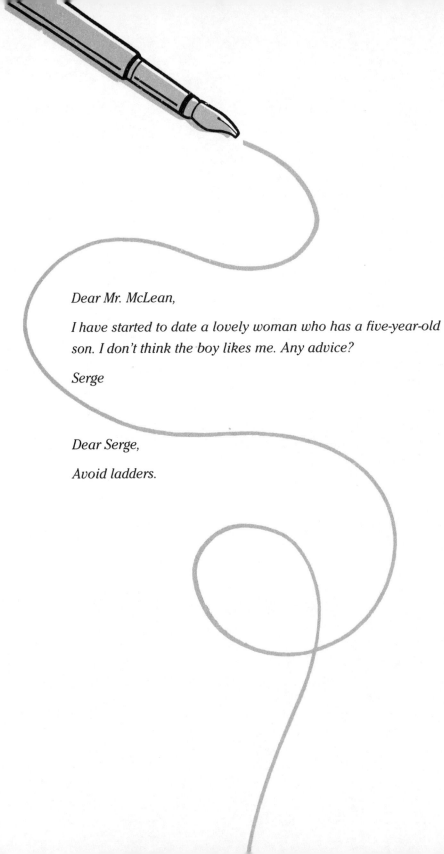

Dear Mr. McLean,

I have started to date a lovely woman who has a five-year-old son. I don't think the boy likes me. Any advice?

Serge

Dear Serge,

Avoid ladders.

SPRING IN THE NARROWS

A few springs ago, when Dave's mother, Margaret, was going through a bad spot, feeling old and overwhelmed, Dave flew home to Cape Breton Island for a weekend to give her a hand with the things that need a hand when the seasons are changing. He went on a Thursday night and stayed until Sunday afternoon.

While he was there, Dave took down the storm windows and put up the screens. He turned the garden, raked the twigs off the lawn and cleaned out the eaves. In the evenings, he walked with his mother into town to buy ice cream. He stopped in at the Maple Leaf Restaurant on Saturday morning and had breakfast with some childhood friends. And each night, he stretched out on his childhood bed in his old room at the top of the stairs, and he slept like a boy, deep and far away. When he left that Sunday, he left thinking that this was something he should have been doing for years.

Since that spring, Dave has made the flight home twice a year, once every April to lay things out, and then again in October to pack them away. It makes him feel useful; connected to things gone by and to the swing of the seasons. He knows his mother looks forward to these visits. He likes that too.

So Dave was surprised, to say the least, the spring he stepped out of his rented car onto his mother's gravel driveway in the little town of Big Narrows, to see she had hired a man, and the two of them were working away at the windows without him.

The man, his white hair wispy and whipping in the wind, was up the old wooden ladder, with a bucket hooked on the top rung, washing the windows of Dave's sister's old bedroom. His mother, with a rag and bucket of her own, was working on a pile of storm windows propped against the front porch.

"David!" she said, as he stepped out of the car, her rag dangling by her side.

He had taken an early plane, and his sweet time on the drive from Sydney, choosing the old road along the St. Andrew's Channel. He had stopped for a coffee and sandwich in Irish Bay, eating it outside even though it was uncomfortably windy for that.

"It's David," Margaret said to the man on the ladder, stomping toward Dave in her Wellingtons, big wet splotches on her olive-coloured pants.

It felt good to be out of the rental car, the wind on his face again. Dave hugged his mother.

"How was your flight?" she asked.

They walked away from the car together, instinctively heading toward the garden, which Dave was surprised to see had already been turned. He pointed at the cold frame, at the little tomato seedlings pumping away.

"You've been busy," he said.

"Smith's been helping," said Margaret.

"Smith," called Margaret, again, "it's David."

The man came down the ladder effortlessly, almost carelessly, as if he had been living on ladders all his life. It was hard to tell how old he was, but he was older up close than he was coming down the ladder, that's for sure.

He was wearing a beige canvas jacket, with a grey fisherman's sweater under it. The jacket was frayed at the cuffs and had clips instead of buttons. Dave was shaking the man's hand, trying to remember where he had heard his name before, and coveting the jacket all at once.

"Nice of you to help out," said Dave.

Then he remembered. This wasn't a hired hand. This was the retired fire chief. This was the guy who had sealed up his mother's laundry chute.

"Get your stuff out of the car," said Margaret. "Supper is nearly ready. I have a chicken going."

Dave took his suitcase upstairs, threw it onto his bed and walked to the window. With the trees still not in bud, he could see all the way down to the storefronts on Railroad Street— the steeple on the United Church at one end, and the tallest building in town, the clock tower on the town hall, at the other. He leaned into the window, letting his breath fog the glass. Everything was still the same. The view from the window was the same view he had had when he was a boy. There was no other place in the world where time had stopped like it had here.

He turned suddenly, went into his old clothes closet and reached up behind the door frame. There was a hole in the plaster the size of a grapefruit. He stood on his toes and reached into the hole, searching with his hand. He smiled and pulled out a purple Crown Royal bag. He took the bag to his bed, reached into it and pulled out his complete set of Parkhurst hockey cards: 1957 to 1958.

He lay on his bed and thumbed through the cards.

There were only two teams in the set. The Canadiens and the Leafs. Fifty cards in all. He took the thick brown elastic band from around them. Doug Harvey, the great Montreal defenceman, was card number *1*; then the man who invented the slapshot, "Boom Boom" Geoffrion. Jean Beliveau, who could have been Governor General, was next; then Henri Richard, followed by his brother, card number *5*, the great Maurice "The Rocket" Richard.

The texture of the paper, so thick it was almost cardboard, was unlike anything they use today. And the inks—the primary blues, the dramatic reds and the vibrant yellow accents—were like a whisper in his ear: the siren song of his boyhood calling him, down the kaleidoscope of memory, to the schoolyard, a-bustle with boys, all of them trading and flipping cards like carnival barkers.

Yo-yos and chestnuts. Stems and strings. Frogs in the creek. Tadpoles in a jar. Red-winged blackbirds and squirrels. His old red bike.

He sat up and put the cards on his bedside table. He spent the next ten minutes unpacking his bag. He put everything into the empty top drawer of his old bureau. It was like settling into a hotel room. Another chance to start again. Another chance at a life where you hang up your shirts and fold everything neatly. When he had finished unpacking, he put the hockey cards back in the liquor bag and the bag back in the wall.

When Dave went downstairs, Smith Gardner was washing his hands in the kitchen sink. Dave saw him glance at the empty towel rack beside the fridge. Dave, still on the stairs, made to fetch a towel, but before he took even a step, Smith reached for the second drawer to the right of the stove, pulled out a fresh towel and shook it open. This was clearly not the first time Smith Gardner had washed his hands at that sink.

Dave glanced at the kitchen table. It was set for three.

"I invited Smith to stay," said Margaret.

Margaret sat down in the chair where she always sat, the chair close to the stove. For the last few years Dave had been sitting in the spot where his father, Charlie, used to sit, to Margaret's right. That chair had a place set in front of it. But so did the chair where Dave sat when he was a boy. Dave saw Smith glance at the table, and it occurred to him he didn't want to sit in his boyhood chair, not if Smith Gardner was in his father's.

He didn't actually run across the kitchen. But he did lurch. He lurched across the kitchen, beat Smith to the table, sat down in his father's place and then looked at Smith, half stood up again and said, "I'm not in *your* seat, am I?"

Smith said, "I don't have a seat."

But Dave didn't miss the glance that passed between his mother and this man.

Dinner, as always, was plentiful. There was chicken and mashed potatoes, and a bowl of peas (canned), and a bowl of squash (fresh), and a plate of bread, and butter, and a cabbage salad.

As they passed things around, Smith said, "My son and I were trying to work out if he had played hockey against you."

"Against me?" said Dave.

"He played for Port Hawkesbury," said Smith. "Right wing."

Dave said, "I don't think we had a town team."

He looked at his mother.

"You weren't on it," she said.

"What about baseball?" said Smith, reaching for the butter. "Didn't the Narrows win the provincial cup a couple times back then?"

Dave shrugged. "Not when I was on the team."

There was an awkward silence. As if it was obvious that that was no coincidence.

Margaret raised her eyebrows. Margaret said to Smith, "Tell David about your house." She turned to Dave. "He built it himself," she said.

"Oh," said Dave. He was remembering his disastrous attempt to rewire a kitchen outlet. Maybe a whole house was easier.

Soon enough dinner was over. Soon enough the dishes were done, and Smith was standing by the back door.

"Margaret," he said, "that was delicious." He turned to go, but before he was out the door, he turned back and said, "Are we going to the church thing tomorrow night?"

Dave picked up a crossword book from the coffee table and pretended he wasn't listening.

Dave is not by nature a morning person. He wakes up slowly and, almost always, later than he would like. The long flight east, the shift in time zones, the bed of his boyhood—all of these things worked on him that night. He meant to be up at seven. It was 8:30 when the slap of the ladder on his bedroom window jerked him awake. When he opened his eyes, there was Smith Gardner at the window, peering in at him.

He swung his legs over the edge of the bed and sat up stupidly. Smith was struggling with the outside storm window.

"Morning," called Smith cheerily.

Dave felt humiliated. He had planned to be up long before this. He staggered to the window. The window appeared stuck.

"Let me help," said Dave.

He gave the window a mighty thump.

Smith's eyes bulged as the window flew toward him unexpectedly. And then, propelled by the suddenly loose window, the ladder tipped back ever so slightly.

Smith, who now had one hand on the ladder and one on the window, hovered there for a moment, and then, just like the coyote in the Road Runner cartoons, in exquisite cartoon slow motion, Smith tipped back and vanished from view, clutching the storm window as he disappeared.

Dave galloped downstairs and flew out the back door.

The ladder was on the ground. But Smith and the window were nowhere to be seen.

"Smith?" called Dave.

Dave heard a rustle above him, like the flapping of bird wings or a moth buffeting a lamp. He looked up.

Smith was dangling above him, one hand clutching the

eavestrough, the other still holding the unstuck storm. His legs were windmilling wildly.

Dave wrestled the ladder up and shoved it against the side of the house. Smith managed to get his feet onto it. Then, with one hand still gripping the window, Smith shimmied down the rungs. When his feet hit the ground, Dave apologized. Smith stared at him, handed him the window and headed for the kitchen door.

"No problem. Thanks for the help," he muttered as he disappeared inside.

That night Dave set the bedside alarm for 7:30. He woke the next morning at 7:15, to a percussive *thumpa! thumpa! thumpa!* He squinted at the clock and groaned. He swung his feet over the bed and staggered to the window. Smith Gardner was standing at the edge of the garden with his back to Dave. There was a pile of one-by-threes on the ground beside him and a sledgehammer at his feet. He was using a nail gun to erect a fence around the vegetable patch.

"We want to keep the deer out this summer," said Margaret when Dave struggled through the kitchen.

We? thought Dave as he headed out the door, doing up his belt on the fly. We *want to keep the deer out?*

Smith and Dave worked together for most of the morning, Dave fetching and holding pickets for the fence, Smith driving the nails. At noon Smith surveyed the sky and said, "I think we could paint it this afternoon."

Dave said, "Why don't you go get the paint and I'll finish it off."

Dave held his hand out for the nail gun. But Smith didn't move. He stared at Dave, the gun dangling beside his thigh. Dave reached for it. Smith tightened his grip. Dave, who now had his hand on the gun, gave it a little tug. Smith looked at Dave with reluctance. He could see the scene unfolding—two little boys wrestling over their favourite toy. Smith let go. But he didn't leave. He stood there.

"Go on," said Dave. "Get the paint."

Dave held the nail gun up, the long plastic strip of nails dangling down to his knees.

He ran his hand along the gun. He had never actually used a nail gun before. He wanted to say, *This is the trigger, right?* But he didn't want to appear stupid. So he didn't ask. Unfortunately.

Instead Dave hefted the gun and touched the trigger tentatively. The gun went off. Three quick rounds. *Thumpa! Thumpa! Thumpa!*

The volley of nails flew across the lawn.

"Woah," said Smith. "Careful."

"Don't worry," said Dave. He turned toward Smith, smiling with what he hoped was benign calm. He was feeling anything but calm. He was shaken by the explosion, so shaken, in fact, that he forgot that his finger was still squeezing the trigger. He turned toward Smith to reassure and apologize. Smith threw himself to the ground and covered his head, just as the next barrage of nails exploded from the gun. The nails whizzed across the yard, barely clearing the white wisps of hair on Smith's head.

One shattered the back window of Smith's gleaming pickup. It lodged in the dashboard like an arrow. Another punctured his rear right tire. Then the gun, blessedly, was empty.

As the air hissed out of the tire, Smith scrambled to his feet. He looked over at his ruined truck and then back at Dave. Smith reached out his hand and snatched the gun back from Dave.

As Dave let go of the gun, he tried to look thoughtful.

"It's really quite responsive, isn't it?" he said.

Everyone tried their best to be upbeat at lunch, but there was no denying the tension at the table. When Dave came into the kitchen, Margaret and Smith were standing by the sink whispering. When Dave made tea, he saw Smith sniff it suspiciously.

After lunch the two of them went outside and settled into separate jobs. Smith went at the new fence with a paintbrush. Dave used his father's old axe to attack the cord of wood by the shed.

He was out of practice and, as the afternoon wore on, he became painfully aware that Smith was outpacing him. He was determined not to fall behind. So Dave sped up. Soon Dave was cracking away at the wood like a maniac.

Smith glanced over at him, anxiety creasing his brow. Smith sped up too, working his way down the fence as fast as he could, trying to paint his way out of range of Dave's flying axe.

Before long they had worked each other into a frenzy: Smith slopping paint on the fence, while Dave, his shirt off, bobbed up and down in front of the woodpile like a mechanical woodpecker.

"Oh my goodness," said Margaret when she came out with tea.

The two of them stopped and stared at her dumbly, both of them panting like sweaty weasels.

"Tea?" said Margaret.

Safe upstairs, Dave leaned against the bathroom window and tried to pull himself together. Below him in the yard, a worried-looking Smith Gardner was saying something to Margaret. She reached out and patted his arm gently. The same way she used to pat Dave and his sister Annie when they were upset.

He couldn't believe this was happening to him—his own mother, in his own house, with another man.

The next morning, Saturday, Margaret put the question of Smith on the table.

"This is silly," she said. "At my age. It's a mistake. I can't change things around at this stage of my life."

Dave, who had never been in the position of giving his mother dating advice, didn't know what to say. He froze up and a silence fell between them.

Dave said, "I'll do the dishes."

He was muttering to himself as he scrubbed intensely around the inside of a pot. He should have said something.

On Sunday morning Dave said, "I think I'll go for a walk."

"It's chilly," said Margaret.

"I'll be okay," said Dave.

He took a black sweater off a peg in the mud room. The sweater used to be his father's. He went out the back door and stood on the lawn. It was one of those perfect spring mornings, a morning that would make anyone who had gone away and come back wonder why they had left in the first place.

Margaret was right, it was chilly, but the sun was shining and it would warm up soon enough. He headed down the hill toward town.

Little rivers trickled into the ditch beside the road. Dave missed the sogginess of spring. He watched a hawk circling over the creek. As he rounded the corner just before his cousin, Colm McDougall's, place, a red-winged blackbird flapped off a telephone pole and coughed its way toward Macaulay's maple bush. The dust of summer, like the dust of days gone by, seemed far away.

When he got to town, Dave stopped in at the Maple Leaf Restaurant for a coffee. It still came in a white porcelain mug with a matching creamer. He sat at the counter, thinking about nothing at all. Pretty soon he was remembering the times he had sat there with his father; he and Charlie sharing an order of french fries after a ball game, a movie or, don't tell your mother, dinner. Oh Charlie. When Dave finished his coffee, he chatted to Alice at the cash, and then wandered along Railway Street.

He passed Art Gillespie's old laundromat and ice plant, and Kerrigan's Foods. He remembered the year he had built the one-sided float for the Narrows' Christmas parade. Dave had been trying to impress what's her name—Megan Lorius. He hadn't thought about her for years; he was so stuck on her. She was so stuck up.

Dave, lost in thought, was no longer paying attention to where he was going. Didn't know he was going anywhere.

He wandered past Kerrigan's and out the south end of town. He stopped on the Thamesville Bridge and leaned on the rusty green rail and watched the current, picking out bubbles on the water surface and following them as far as he could.

It was the very same spot where Charlie and he had stood the summer he was eleven years old. The afternoon Charlie had taught him how to jump. All his friends had already done it, but Dave was afraid.

They were on their way home from church, dressed in their Sunday best.

"Hold my hand," said Charlie. "We'll go together."

"Mom's going to kill us," said Dave when they surfaced.

"I know," said Charlie, splashing toward the riverbank. "Isn't it grand?"

Charlie always had believed in his son. Despite all evidence to the contrary, Charlie had believed Dave could do anything.

Dave came to, standing by the stone gates of the Big Narrows Union Cemetery.

The Union Cemetery is in a little square clearing where the Gillespie Road ends in a T-junction with the road to the Macaulays' place. If you are in a car, you have to turn left or right at the stop sign, but if you are walking, like Dave was, you can keep going and walk straight into the graveyard. Which is what Dave did.

He walked into the graveyard and along the gravel path about halfway to the back, and then he left the path and cut across the grass.

He didn't go to his father's grave first. First he went to the far corner of the graveyard, where the hill dips away and the trees are old and big. To where the graves are shaded, and there are pine needles instead of grass.

There was, unbelievably, still a mound of snow by the fence. This was the corner where the old graves were. As Dave wandered among them, his fingers brushed absentmindedly against the stones.

Many of the inscriptions, worn by winter wind and rain, were too faded to read anymore. Some of the stones barely poked out of the earth, as if the ground was rising up to swallow them.

For dust thou art and unto dust shalt thou return.

He walked across to a newer section and found his father's stone and stood in front of it, wearing the black sweater his dad used to wear when he worked in the yard.

Hey, he said silently. *How are you doing?*

Then he said, *Mom has a boyfriend. I mean. I think she has a boyfriend.*

Yeah, she has a boyfriend. And I don't know what I am supposed to think about that.

I was wondering what you were thinking. I am assuming you already know.

Dave looked over at the old trees.

I keep thinking of you up here by yourself. I keep thinking of you all alone. I don't want you to be lonely. And I wanted to know that you were, you know, I don't know. Are you okay? Are you okay with this?

Maybe, he said, *if you had looked after yourself, we wouldn't be in this mess.*

Then he said, *Sorry. I love you.*

He was still standing there, feeling sorry, when a green pickup pulled onto the gravel by the gates. When he looked over, Dave saw Smith Gardner step out of the cab and walk through the gates. He was carrying a weed whacker.

When Smith saw Dave he stopped abruptly. Dave was by the grave, Smith by the gates. Dave looked awkward. Smith looked … nervous?

"Hey," said Dave. "It's okay." *Did Smith think he was going to injure him here?*

Smith walked over.

"I didn't expect to run into you," said Smith.

"I didn't expect to come," said Dave.

Smith looked down at the stone. "Is this Charlie?" he asked.

Dave nodded.

"I've never been here," said Smith. "I mean I've been here plenty. Too often these days. But never to see him."

He held up the weed whacker and motioned at the grave.

"Doesn't seem to need it."

The two of them stood there for a moment and then Smith said, "I never met him."

"He was a good guy," said Dave. "He liked music."

"I know," said Smith. "So does your mom. They used to sing."

Dave smiled. "She told you?"

"Oh," said Smith. "She's told me all about him. All about him.

"I don't know anything about music myself. I got the lowest score in music in all of Port Hawkesbury when I was a young-ster. The opera? I don't know even a little bit about that. I haven't the foggiest how to talk to her about it." He shook his head. "So I just listen and nod."

He was wringing his hands. Then he cleared his throat and

said the most stunning thing. He said, "I thought of asking her to marry me, but I'm terrified she would make me dance with her at the wedding."

Dave didn't blink. Without thinking, not for a moment, Dave said, "You'd be fine. You could take lessons. Or not. You don't have to dance." It came out fast, in an awkward rush.

They stared at each other as what they had both said sank in.

Smith was the one who changed the subject. "It is his birthday next weekend," said Smith, nodding at Charlie's stone.

"He would have been eighty-eight," said Dave.

"Eighty-seven," said Smith.

Smith held up the weed whacker. "I thought your mother would want to come by. I thought I would drop by first and clean it up a bit, clip the grass, you know. Whatever." He looked self-conscious. He held out the weed whacker. "Maybe you'd like to do it. It's not that bad, really."

An hour later, on his way back through town, Dave stopped in at the library. He wanted to use the computers. He wanted to send an email to Morley.

Interesting day. I went out to the cemetery and Smith showed up. The guy I was telling you about. I think he asked me for permission to marry my mother. I think I told him it was okay. I didn't mean to. I am not even sure if that's what happened. To tell you the truth, I don't have a clue how I feel.

Though I can tell you I miss Dad.

I think all I want is for Dad to tell me he is okay with this.

Of course that's what everyone here wants me to tell them.
I guess it is. I'll be home tomorrow night. I booked a flight
this morning.

His fingers were flying across the keys now.

I just wanted to let you know it has been strange here, and I
miss you, and I live you.

That was a typo. He'd meant to write love. He'd meant to write, *I love you.*

I am lucky you are in my life. And I don't think I say that
enough.

He leaned back and sighed and stared at the screen, his hands behind his head. Then he lurched forward abruptly and pressed *Send* without reading another word. He was afraid if he did, he might change it.

Dear Stuart,

Recently, I find myself constantly worrying about being laid off from my job. Over the years, I've followed your career with both interest and amazement. You seem to have hung on to your jobs for a surprisingly long time, especially considering, well, considering your lack of what are traditionally considered "skills." Can you share with me the secret of your longevity?

Truly,
Sarah

Dear Sarah,

I suppose the secret of my current career success is that I am self-employed—and my boss is pretty clueless about what is going on. Some people I know, however, have found that having strong and resourceful allies at their place of work seems to help. You might find the attached story of some interest.

WALLY

For as long as anyone can remember, and for reasons no one can recall, William Jarvis has been known as Wally to the teachers, the parents and the children at Sam's school—the *only* person from the galaxy of adults addressed by his first name in the cosmos of kids.

Wally the janitor, Wally the caretaker, world-famous Wally; overalled, wool-capped and, more often than not, unshaven Wally. Wally, who is best known, and most loved, for the lunch hour every April when he climbs up onto the school roof. With every kid from kindergarten to grade eight gathered below him, all of them howling with delight, Wally balances, like a knight on a castle turret, on the very edge of the school roof, and tosses down, one after the other, an entire year of roofed tennis balls.

The first spring Wally did this, there was a never-ending supply of balls up there, and Wally leaned back before each throw, hurling balls with abandon while the kids chanted and cheered. Nearly every kid got a ball that spring. But that was because no one had been up on the roof for years.

The past few years, the supply has been so scarce that Wally has actually gone out and bought balls to augment what he finds up there. To give them roof-like authenticity, Wally

~ 51 ~

and his wife age the new balls the week before the big event. They soak them in a mixture of mud and cold tea.

On *ball day*, as it is called, Wally always keeps a couple of balls in his pockets, and when he climbs down from the roof, he slips them to little kids who would be trampled if they joined the schoolyard stampede.

Wally is from New Brunswick. His father was a fisherman, and his father's father before that. Wally was going to be a fisherman too; he used to set traps with his grandfather when he was a boy. But the fishery collapsed. And Wally ended up cleaning windows in the city, dangling over the edge of office towers in a body harness. He didn't mind it. It wasn't any different from being hauled up a mast to unfoul a halyard. And he still got to work with water. And on windy days you got bounced around up there, just like being out in the bay.

But it was lonely work.

Sometimes Wally would tap on a window, and pull a face, or wave. And the office workers would smile and hold up their mugs of coffee. And every day you could count on *someone* waving at you and inviting you in. But Wally couldn't go in, of course. All Wally could do was wave back and winch himself out of sight.

But that is how he met his wife.

She was one of the women who worked in one of those offices. She thought Wally looked so sweet working away, and all the other women said she should do *something* about that, and one day she did. She held up one of her homemade banana muffins and William grinned and pointed down at the street, and darned if at the end of the day she wasn't waiting at the bottom of his rope with a muffin. They got married six months later.

So it wasn't *totally* lonely. Wally stuck at window washing for twelve years. He didn't *mind* the job. But he didn't *love* it. He *loved* his job at the school.

Not everyone in the world is cut out to be a school janitor. A lot of people would be worn down by the spilled paint, the vomit and the gum-stuck floors.

Not Wally. Wally *loved* it.

Every day was different. There was always some happy kid bringing him a birthday cupcake wrapped in wax paper. Or some kid with troubles. Wally had a special feel for the kids with troubles. He is the only one in the school who Mark Portnoy, schoolyard bully and classroom nuisance, will listen to.

One year, on the last afternoon of school, a Friday afternoon in June, the June Mark was in grade four, Wally found Mark's art folder in the garbage. An entire year's worth of art. Wally saved it—until school was back in September.

"You should've taken this home to your mother," said Wally.

Mark Portnoy snorted. "What?" said Mark. "So *she* could throw it out? I saved her the trouble."

Wally began to flip through the portfolio page by page. Mark stayed and watched. He said, "This is stupid." But he didn't leave. Wally set aside three pictures.

Wally said, "I'm putting these up in my office."

Mark said, "That's your problem."

It was the first time *anyone* had put *anything* Mark did up on a wall.

The next year, on the last day of school, Mark Portnoy *brought* his art file to Wally.

He said, "I don't need this junk."

Wally went through it again, choosing three more pictures while Mark stood and watched.

Wally just might be the *perfect* school janitor. And then one day, he vanished. One day the kids came to school and Wally was gone. There was an old man in his place. No one knew his name, or where he had come from. But they knew one thing: He was a disaster. They knew that right from the first morning.

Everyone sat in class that morning watching him in horror. There he was, his first day, down on his hands and knees in the middle of the schoolyard, poking at the schoolyard drain. There was a pickaxe and a snake on the ground beside him.

The schoolyard drain had been blocked for years. Wally had never gone near it. Wally understood the *blessings* of a blocked drain. Wally understood the pleasures of puddles; the slipperiness of ice.

At recess everyone tore outside. The grade sevens organized the grade ones to stand on the drain so the new janitor couldn't get at it. There was a standoff that lasted a good five minutes before the new janitor picked up his stuff and went inside. As soon as he was gone, a group of girls began to scoop up the salt he had dumped on the ice around the drain, while the grade-six boys organized kids to bring water.

It was Sam's best friend, Murphy, who got on the case. It was Murphy who went to the office and asked about Wally outright, Murphy who brought the news back to the other boys.

"Wally was made redundant," said Murphy.

There were four boys standing in the boys' bathroom listening to Murphy's report. Peter Moore was the first to speak. Peter said, "That's gross."

Gregory said, "Is it fatal?"

"It doesn't sound good," said Murphy. "Mr. Lovell said the union is grieving."

"It *is* fatal," said Gregory.

Murphy tried to talk to the principal, Mrs. Cassidy, after school. Mrs. Cassidy was late for a parent meeting. Mrs. Cassidy didn't even stop moving. "He is not with us anymore," she said, adding over her shoulder, "It's been pretty brutal. There's been some serious slashing."

Mr. Miller, the vice-principal, confirmed it. "He has been cut."

Murphy carried the news back to the boys' room.

"It's worse than we thought," said Murphy.

"What are we going to do?" said Sam.

"I don't know," said Murphy. "I've got to think about it."

Then, that very night, on his way home from dinner at his grandparents', Murphy, alone in the back of his parents' car and almost asleep, opened his eyes as they passed the school. Murphy opened his eyes and saw him.

"It was *him*," said Murphy.

They were back in the boys' washroom. Murphy, Sam, Peter, Geoff and Gregory.

Murphy said, "He was hunched over and moving really slowly."

"You saw him?" said Gregory.

"His shadow," said Murphy. "I saw his shadow. It was huge against the wall, and he was all bent over."

"Why would he be all bent over?" said Peter.

Geoff punched him. Geoff said, "Because he has been cut up and made redundant, stupid."

"I knew that," said Peter.

And then Peter, who was getting afraid, said, "Where do you think they keep him during the day?"

Geoff said, "In the supply cupboard. With all the other redundant people.

"That's why they keep it locked," said Geoff. "They let them out at night, and they roam the halls."

Everyone was nodding. Except Murphy. Murphy was shaking his head.

Murphy said, "The boiler room."

Peter looked horrified. Peter said, "All those weird noises...."

Geoff said, "The clanging and the moans."

Murphy nodded. Murphy said, "It's the redundant people."

Sam got a note from Murphy in the middle of math class. Which wouldn't be noteworthy, except Murphy isn't in Sam's math class.

Meet me in the locker room after school.

When Sam arrived, Murphy was staring at the rusted door that led into the sub-basement. And from there, to the boiler room.

Murphy said, "We have to get in there."

Sam, who had heard about the boiler room but had never actually seen it, said, "I was afraid of that."

The two of them were standing in front of the locked door, when it opened suddenly, and the new janitor walked out.

He looked at the boys and frowned. "You don't want to go in *there*, boys. Boys could get hurt in there."

Sam wanted to run. Murphy stood his ground. He was staring at the janitor.

The janitor reached self-consciously behind him and checked he had locked the door.

"Told you," said Murphy, when he was out of earshot.

"Poor Wally," said Sam. "We *have* to do something."

"We will," said Murphy.

Murphy, who could arrange to get a note to a friend in a math class when he was nowhere near the classroom, is not a boy who favours doorbells. When Murphy comes to call, he comes on the wind: a handful of dirt chucked at a window, the hoot of an owl, or, as he came that night, a flashlight beaming from a garage roof.

Sam was already in bed when the flashlight played across his bedroom ceiling.

He went to his window and peered into the night. He couldn't see anything, but he knew.

He flicked his bedroom lights, on and off, off and on. And then he slipped into a pair of sweatpants and out of his room. On his way past his parents' bedroom, he stopped to listen to his father's rhythmic breathing.

Murphy was in his backyard, sitting at the picnic table.

Sam slipped out the back door. "What's going on?"

"I went and checked," said Murphy. "It *is* him. I saw him."

"What are we going to do?" said Sam.

"Tomorrow night," said Murphy. "We are going to free him."

Murphy pulled his hand out of his pocket. His fist was clenched. Slowly Murphy uncurled his fingers. He was holding a key.

Sam shut his eyes and rocked back and forth.

"The boiler room?" said Sam.

It was part question. But mostly it was a statement. Sam already knew the answer.

Five minutes later Sam snuck into his bedroom and five minutes after that he was lying in bed. He lay there for about ten minutes, too keyed up to sleep. After ten minutes he got up and rummaged around in his bureau. He found what he was looking for in the back of the bottom drawer: his old Spider-Man pyjamas. He hadn't worn them for years. He put them on and stood in front of the mirror. The pants came only halfway down his legs. His arms were way too long for the sleeves. But he liked the way they looked.

He got onto his desk the way he used to and leapt onto his bed. He lay there in the darkness.

"I have radioactive blood," he said.

When the school board cut back on its custodial staff, Wally was too far down the seniority list to hold on to his day shift at Sam's school. The board offered him a day position across town, but Wally opted to take the night shift at the school he loved. It seemed like a good choice at the time, but a month into the job, Wally was regretting it. The night shift was lonely. Lonelier, even, than window washing. The school felt unnatural at night—as hollow as an empty amusement park. And on the odd night when there were people inside the building, they were never kids. The people were nothing but an irritant. A week ago there was a staff meeting that dragged on and on, and Wally had to stay an hour later than usual. Tonight a neighbourhood committee was meeting to discuss speed limits, and traffic flow, and whether or not the street lights were turning on at the right time of night.

Wally knew that he would have to interrupt them several times before they would clear out, and that whatever he did, there would be stragglers preventing him from locking up and getting home on time.

Sam and Murphy didn't know *anything* about any of that. All Sam and Murphy knew was that Wally was in trouble. And that they had to do something.

According to the plan, they were to meet in the schoolyard. At the top of the slide. When everyone was asleep.

Sam lay in bed staring at the clock, willing it to move, praying it wouldn't, until, all of a sudden, it was time. He got up and dressed and carefully arranged a pile of laundry under his blankets the way Murphy had told him, trying to make it appear as if he was tucked in bed, asleep. Then he snuck downstairs and slid out the back door.

He stayed off the sidewalks. He cut across front yards. He climbed over back fences. He kept to the shadows.

He was wearing a backpack. He had packed a flashlight, a penknife, two peanut butter sandwiches, a piece of rope, a Baggie of dog biscuits in case there were dogs, and a book to identify animal spoor.

It was the middle of the night when he got to the school-yard. At least ten o'clock. Maybe even 10:15. And when he got there, he couldn't believe his eyes. There were cars in the parking lot. And there were lights on in the school.

Someone must have squealed on them.

Murphy was already there, waiting.

Murphy said, "I have been here for an hour."

Sam pointed at the lights and the cars. "The people...." said Sam.

But Murphy was already under way. Murphy was half crouched and zigzagging his way across the schoolyard like a commando. Sam ran after him, trying to catch up. Sam didn't want to be alone.

The side door of the school was mysteriously open.

"Come on," said Murphy in the darkness. Sam could hear Murphy, but he couldn't see him.

They came out into a hall at the back of the staff room. There were people talking.

"Shhh," said Murphy. "It's them."

"Who?" said Sam.

"The people who make you redundant."

Sam crept forward and peeked around the open door. He had never seen any of these people in his life.

There was a man saying something.

"It happened again last night," said the man, "somebody is going to get killed one of these days."

Murphy looked at Sam.

"See," said Murphy. "It's them."

"What are we going to do?" asked Sam.

It was Murphy, who had done morning announcements three times already that year, who got them into the vice-principal's office and onto the school public address system. It was Murphy, who sat at the vice-principal's desk and flicked on the PA. It was Murphy who then leaned into the microphone, lowered his voice and did his best Darth Vader impression:

"It is time for you to go. Leave now while you still can."

Then he sat back.

Neither he nor Sam heard the ripple of laughter in the staff room—where the neighbourhood traffic committee had been arguing about speed bumps for the past two and a half hours.

Murphy and Sam were out of earshot. Murphy made his announcement, leaned back and shrugged at Sam. Then he moved toward the microphone once more for good measure:

"You are free to go … if you go *now*."

Murphy flicked off the PA, and he and Sam ran out of the office and down the hall, ducking into Miss Perriton's kindergarten class. They flew to the window. When they saw the cars pulling out of the parking lot, they high-fived each other.

"Let's go," said Sam.

"Not yet," said Murphy. "Wait till the last one."

And so they waited in the dark kindergarten room. And while they waited, they drifted over to the big blocks and built a tower, and the tower became a castle, and soon they forgot why they were there. Murphy was defending the castle against the black knights who had begun an attack with their ally—a monstrous stuffed bear—when suddenly the light in the corridor snapped on and they just about jumped out of their skins.

Sam ran to the window and stared at the parking lot. He mouthed the word *Empty*. They hid in the corner of the classroom and waited.

They waited forever. And nothing happened.

And then ... Wally walked slowly down the hall pushing a broom. They waited another five minutes. Then they went looking for him. But he had vanished.

Wally's office is in the boiler room. Murphy used his key to open the boiler-room door. It was dark and gloomy in there. The ceiling was low and the corridor narrow. There were pipes everywhere—on the walls and on the ceiling. It was like a dungeon.

Murphy said, "Come on."

Wally was sitting at his desk beside the boiler. He had his feet on a milk crate. He was eating a banana muffin. He had a stainless steel Thermos beside him.

They stood in the doorway for maybe a minute without saying anything. Wally didn't see them at first. And then he must have sensed them staring at him, and he glanced up and saw the two of them standing there in the gloom.

The sight of them should have startled him, but after you spend twelve years hanging over the edge of high-rises day in and day out, you don't startle easily.

Wally put his muffin down, pulled his feet off the milk crate and waved them in.

"Hello boys," he said. "Was that you on the PA?"

Murphy nodded. He reached into his pocket and pulled out the key.

Murphy stepped forward, held out the key and said, "You're free to go now."

Wally looked stunned.

Murphy whispered to Sam, "It will take awhile for him to recover from the redundancy."

"It's okay," said Murphy. "They've gone."

"All of them?" asked Wally. "They're not hanging around the doors?"

"All of them," said Sam. "You're safe. You can go."

"About time," said Wally, glancing at his watch.

He wanted to walk them home. But they went alone.

"We're okay," said Murphy.

"Did you see how fast he wanted to get out of there?" said Sam.

They were in Sam's backyard, sitting at the picnic table again.

"Swear you'll never tell," said Murphy.

"I swear," said Sam.

They shook hands.

Five minutes later Sam was pulling on his Spider-Man pyjamas when he froze in horror. The pile of laundry he had stuffed under his covers was piled neatly on his desk chair. He stared at his bed in the darkness. He took a deep breath and let it out slowly.

The lump in his bed moved. "Hi," it said.

"Hi," said Sam.

It was his father.

Neither of them said anything for a moment. Then Sam said, "I can't tell you what I have been doing."

"You take an oath?" said Dave.

"Yes," said Sam.

"Must have been very important to keep you up so late," said Dave.

"Yes," said Sam.

"Everything okay?" said Dave.

"Yes," said Sam. "Everything's fine."

"Is everyone okay?" said Dave.

"Yes."

"Is everyone at home? In bed?"

Dave was sitting on the edge of the bed staring at his son.

Sam said, "Soon."

"I've been pretty worried," said Dave.

Sam said, "Does Mom know?"

Dave said, "She is sound asleep."

Sam exhaled slowly, and then he crawled into bed with his father.

They lay there in the darkness, and then Dave said, "Can you tell me anything?"

Sam smiled and said, "One thing."

Sam reached out and pulled his father's ear to his mouth. He whispered, "I have radioactive blood."

Wally reappeared on day shift about a month later. The ongoing battle over the drain, not to mention a nasty wave of stomach flu, convinced the new janitor that early retirement wasn't such a bad idea.

Wally came back. And the schoolyard drain is plugged solid again, just the way it should be.

Only a very select circle knows about Sam and Murphy's night in the school; and how they saved Wally from redundancy.

Some boys say it's not true, that they weren't even there.

That's what Mark Portnoy was saying at recess a few weeks ago.

Mark had Murphy pinned against the coatroom wall and was threatening to take his lunch when Wally came along, and Mark had to let Murphy go. Mark thought he would save face by asking Wally outright.

"He says he and snot-nose snuck in here one night and saved you from the recumbent people."

Wally looked quizzically at Murphy and then at Sam, who was there too. Then he looked at Mark Portnoy and said, "As a matter of fact, those people would probably still be in the staff room making their plans if it weren't for those two."

Then he took Mark Portnoy down to his office and gave him a doughnut and some coffee from his Thermos, and Mark forgot about Murphy's lunch. And truth be known, Mark has been treating both Sam and Murphy with what almost passes as respect ever since.

Dear Mr. McLean,

I understand that you travel across this great country with your show The Vinyl Cafe, *so I assume you have seen many of the natural and man-made marvels that this country has to offer. With that in mind, I am wondering if you know where I might locate a porcelain hedgehog?*

Yours truly,

Nigel

Dear Nigel,

Funny you should ask.

LONDON

The ticket arrived like Dorothy always arrives herself, unannounced. It landed, with a slap of presumption, along with the rest of the day's mail, on the kitchen table. A return flight for Stephanie, to London, England, booked and paid for.

"But I just got home," said Stephanie. "I don't want to go away again."

The ticket came in July, just as Stephanie was unpacking from two months of tree planting in the north. It came when she was looking forward to summertime at home—looking forward to reconnecting with her city friends at sidewalk cafés. Looking forward to spending time with her boyfriend, Tommy.

It's time for Stephanie to see more of the world, wrote Dorothy in her abrupt note.

Maybe. But Stephanie took the plane ticket as an affront. What sensible young tree-planter wants to celebrate her return to civilization by spending two weeks with a geriatric aunt, even if that aunt happens to live where civilization's heartbeat pumps like in few other places?

Morley said, "You *have* to go."

Stephanie said, "*Why* do I have to go? It's my life. What has Aunt Dorothy got to do with *my* life?"

The next evening Dave handed her a two-page typed list of places she *had* to see. The Ad Lib Club in Soho's Ham Yard, where he had had a beer with George Harrison. Well, okay, George Harrison was at the next table over. Just before Dave got there.

There were also directions to where the Marquee Club used to be—the club where everyone *except* the Beatles played, where Jimi Hendrix gave his last performance.

"You want me to go to see where the club used to be?" said Stephanie, scanning her father's list. She looked appalled.

"*Everyone* played there," said Dave. "The Yardbirds, Manfred Mann, David Bowie, Cream, Pink Floyd, The Who."

"But *not* the Beatles," said Stephanie.

"No. I mean, yes," said Dave. "That's right. Not the Beatles. But everyone else."

"And," said Stephanie, "you want me to go to London so I can stand on the street where it used to be, and where the Beatles never were."

"To *see* it," said Dave.

"You mean *not* to see it," said Stephanie. "I could go outside right now and not see it, and I wouldn't have to leave home."

When Stephanie, bleary-eyed and rumpled from the overnight flight, lumbered into the Arrivals area at Heathrow, she spotted Aunt Dorothy immediately. Dorothy, in her Clarks Wallabees, and wool skirt, and Marks & Spencer cardigan, was looking at her watch impatiently. "My word," said Dorothy, pointing at Stephanie's bulky suitcase. "Did you think you were coming for a month, dear?"

"Hi," was all Stephanie could think to say in reply.

"Well, never mind," said Dorothy, already on the move. She marched to the parking lot three steps ahead of Stephanie. When they got to her 1967 Vauxhall Viva, Dorothy wrenched Stephanie's suitcase from her hand and hoisted it into the backseat. Then she was rocketing the car out of the parking spot as if there was a national emergency. On her way, she managed to bang into the cars that were both in front of and behind her—which set off the alarm she had installed to warn her when she was too close to the cars around her.

They flew down the motorway, heading for the village of Hawkhurst, about an hour to the southeast of the airport, Dorothy occasionally pounding on the dashboard in vain attempts to silence the alarm.

She barrelled fearlessly along in the fast lane, pounding, until, without any warning, and without much slowing, and certainly without signalling, she exited the motorway onto a one-lane road barely the width of her little car.

"Shortcut," said Dorothy grimly as they crested a hill, actually leaving the ground in the process. She was flying between the hedgerows and around blind corners with no concern *whatsoever* that something might be coming toward her from the opposite direction.

Stephanie did not have time to be frightened. She was hanging on to the door handle, her eyes closed and her lips pressed tight, trying not to be carsick.

Just as she thought she had lost the battle, Dorothy's car cleared a little hill, geared down, turned onto a small gravel road and rocked to a stop before a small country house. "I hope you're hungry," said Dorothy to her pale and shaking niece. "I have a little lunch going."

"A little lunch," it turned out, meant a cow's tongue, simmering in a Crock-Pot with carrots and onions and cabbage.

Stephanie's first text message to Tommy was frantic.

It looked like a tongue. It tasted like a tongue. And, worst of all, it felt like a tongue.

Tommy texted her right back. One word: *Sweet.*

After they had finished lunch, Stephanie, too excited to sleep during the long night flight over the Atlantic, fell into bed—exhausted and nauseated.

She woke the next morning sweating and disoriented.

She wandered into the kitchen and found Dorothy bent over the sink. She was scrubbing an empty Marmite jar with a vegetable brush.

"They've started selling Marmite in tubes," said Dorothy. "Like toothpaste."

This was clearly not something Dorothy thought of as progress.

Dorothy yanked open the cupboard under the sink. There was a box *full* of empty Marmite jars. She added the latest to her collection.

"I squeeze it out of the tubes into the jars," said Dorothy. She shook her head. "Marmite shouldn't come in tubes."

It was after breakfast that the real purpose of Stephanie's trip emerged. Stephanie was sitting at the kitchen table, stunned by the mallet of jet lag.

Dorothy was wiping a Mountbatten memorial teapot with a tea towel.

"I just have a few of these left," she said, referring to her once-vast collection of royal china.

She held the teapot up. There was a piece of white adhesive tape on the bottom. She said, "I have written *your* name on this, dearie. While you're here you can choose what else you want. And help me go through the rest of it."

Dorothy, an only child, never married, and now alone and over seventy, was searching for the comfort of continuity. Dorothy was looking for someone to whom she could pass her life. She had settled on Stephanie.

Stephanie stared at the commemorative teapot, with its gold gilt, and then around the room. She spotted a collection of porcelain hedgehogs, a wire toast rack, an umbrella stand with the Queen Mother's face carved into the front. She couldn't see anything she was remotely interested in possessing. Nothing.

"Thank you," she said, uncertainly.

"We'll deal with my treasures later," said Dorothy. "We have a lot to do. I have our itinerary here. We have to get going."

Stephanie couldn't imagine *anything* Dorothy might want to do that would interest her.

"I have a list of things my father wants me to see," said Stephanie, lamely.

"Never mind that," said Dorothy.

And thus began Stephanie's British education—a tour of London that was more like a forced march. It turned out Dorothy wasn't only concerned with passing along her *things*: She wanted to pass on the glorious wonder of Britain.

They drove into the city and took a small room on the third floor of the quirky and out-of-time Durrants Hotel, just off Marylebone High Street. They checked in, and then marched right out again—onto a series of red double-decker buses that they rode to Bunhill Fields. They stormed past the graves of Daniel Defoe and John Bunyon. They put pebbles on William Blake's grave, in the Jewish tradition.

From Bunhill they headed for Hampstead Heath and the tottering and tangled eccentricity of Highgate Cemetery.

"Karl Marx never even lived in Russia," said Dorothy as they stood in front of the great philosopher's tomb.

As evening fell, they wandered through the winding and hilly neighbourhood of Hampstead.

"That's the house where de Gaulle lived during the war," said Dorothy.

Stephanie had never heard of Charles de Gaulle. She wondered for a beat if this was something she could admit and was about to, but Dorothy was already pounding down the street. "Imagine," said Dorothy as Stephanie scrambled to catch up, "imagine all those men and women waiting for their orders. All those poor boys on bikes."

They were halfway down a hilly green street when Dorothy turned into a laneway.

"This is where John Keats lived," she said.

Stephanie may never have heard of Charles de Gaulle, but she had studied John Keats. "Ode on a Grecian Urn." "Ode to a Nightingale."

"Some of the greatest poems of the English language," said Dorothy, waving her arm in the air. "Written right here. In this very garden."

That night, back in the hotel, Dorothy collapsed into the only armchair in their small room, her mouth hanging open, her head thrown back, snoring rhythmically. Stephanie texted Tommy: *I went to Keats's house. There was a lock of his hair.*

Tommy wrote back immediately, *two* words: *What colour?*

The next morning Dorothy and Stephanie stood in front of a terraced row of Georgian houses not far from the Thames River. Dorothy said, "Has your father told you the story about Carlyle?"

It was chilly. Stephanie was staring glumly at the row of brick houses, wondering if Dorothy was going to drag her to every graveyard and house in London.

"Carl who?" said Stephanie.

"Haven't they taught you anything?" said Dorothy. "It involves one of your ancestors."

The idea that she had ancestors had never occurred to Stephanie. She knew her parents, and she knew her grandparents, but no one had ever said *anything* to her about ancestors.

"Mr. Carlyle was a friend of Mr. John Stuart Mill," said Dorothy. Then she glanced at Stephanie.

Stephanie said, "The philosopher."

Dorothy said, "Good, dearie."

Then she said, "Carlyle took the manuscript of his *History of the French Revolution* to Mr. John Stuart Mill. He wanted him to read it before he sent it to his publisher. Mr. Mill put it down on his desk. The maid found it and thought it was garbage. So she burned it."

"She burned it?" said Stephanie. "What happened?"

"Mr. Carlyle had to write it again. From the beginning."

"And I'm related to John Stuart Mill?" said Stephanie.

"No, no," said Dorothy. "Not Mr. Mill, love. We're related to the maid."

They walked and they walked, and everywhere they walked there was something to see and something to do.

"This is where Lord Byron was born."

"This is the very spot where they executed Anne Boleyn. She was completely unafraid, they say."

"And this is the church where Graham Greene used to confess adultery."

They were standing in a little stone alcove to the right of the chancel. Stephanie was staring at all the flickering candles.

Dorothy said, "Would you like to light a candle?"

"What does it mean?" said Stephanie. "When you light one?"

"I don't know," said Dorothy, "but they look very pretty when they are burning."

Dorothy picked up a taper and started to light candles randomly.

"I think you're supposed to pay," said Stephanie.

"I never pay," said Dorothy. "The Catholics have plenty of money."

They went to Westminster Abbey—to the south transept and the Poets' Corner. A man from Lyons, France, asked Stephanie if she would take his picture standing beside the modest plaque that marked Charles Dickens's grave.

Then they wound their way along the river.

"Everything is so old," said Stephanie.

Dorothy snorted. "Old?" she said. "*This* was all built *after* the Norman invasion."

They wandered past rows and rows of Georgian houses— the houses on one side of the street the mirror image of the houses on the other. Stephanie pointed to a faded S and an arrow, painted on one of the foundations.

"I saw one like that yesterday," she said.

"That's from the war, dearie," said Dorothy. "When Mr. Hitler was dropping bombs on us. It showed you to the shelters."

Then she said, "We used to sleep in the underground."

"The subway stations?" said Stephanie.

They rode the Northern Line to the Camden Town Station.

"This is where I slept," said Dorothy, "right here." She was pointing at a little alcove off the northbound tracks.

Stephanie stood on the gritty platform between the tile wall and the tracks and shivered. It was damp and chilly, and even with the lights on, even in the middle of the day, it was dark down there. Or it felt dark. She wondered what it would have felt like to lie there at night and try to sleep with bombs raining down outside.

"Mother was working at the hospital," said Dorothy. "My job was to come in the afternoon and save a spot."

"How old were you?" said Stephanie.

"Oh, I don't know," said Dorothy, turning to go. "It was a long time ago. I was just a little girl. Maybe seven."

"Where was your father?"

"Father went to the war," said Dorothy. "But I don't know where. He didn't come back. So I never asked him."

She looked at her watch.

"Oh dear," she said. "We have to get up to the Kensington Gardens and pay our respects to Prince Albert."

On their way to see Prince Albert, they stopped and paid their respects to George Orwell, and later, in Trafalgar Square, to Charles I.

They bought a bag of chestnuts.

"Now this," said Dorothy, digging into the bag, "is my favourite statue."

Dorothy finished the last chestnut, scrunched the paper bag up and dropped it on the ground.

"It has been here since 1675," said Dorothy, licking her fingers.

Stephanie waited until Dorothy wasn't looking, bent down quickly and picked up the chestnut bag.

"I come every January," said Dorothy, "for the wreath laying."

"On his birthday?" asked Stephanie, pocketing the paper bag.

"His execution day," said Dorothy, marching off.

The days passed in a whirl. They were up early. They went to bed late. Dorothy never stopped moving.

They walked through parks and gardens; they sat in squares; they waited out rain showers in bookshops. They bought their lunches at little fruit markets. Stephanie eventually gave up trying to work out whether she was hot or cold, or if it was about to rain or clear. She was constantly putting on or taking off her new Marks & Spencer cardigan.

They went to the Royal Stables and saw the carriages, and to the Tower and saw the jewels, and to Hampton Court and to Runnymede. They also went to see where the Marquee Club used to be, where Dave hadn't seen the Beatles.

"Your father is a good man," said Dorothy. Then, to herself, she muttered, "A little off, perhaps."

On their last night in London, they had dinner in a small pub. Cornish pasties: potato, steak, turnip and onion pies.

"My grandfather Charles loved these," said Dorothy. "He took me to the parade on VE day."

"VE day?" said Stephanie.

"Victory in Europe," said Dorothy. "The end of the war."

And then she reached out and said, "You don't eat that part, sweetie."

The half moon–shaped pie had a thick rippled crust. "The Cornish miners used to take these for their lunch. Sometimes they had meat at one end and fruit at the other. The crust was so they could hold them without washing their hands. The crust is just a handle."

Stephanie put the crust down on her plate.

"You were telling me about VE day," said Stephanie.

"We were on the Mall," said Dorothy. "Right across from the royal stand."

"Could you see the queen?" asked Stephanie.

"You mean the king," said Dorothy. "We could see him very easily. Very easily. And Mr. Churchill too. You used to see them all the time. The girls especially. Elizabeth and Margaret. They were always opening gardens and things like that. People seemed to know where they were going to be. There would always be a little crowd. The girls had such beautiful complexions. The English-rose complexion. They were much more beautiful than their photographs. There was not a tremendous amount of security. If you saw a little crowd, you could join in."

"And the parade?" said Stephanie.

"Oh," said Dorothy. "We got there at three in the morning. That's why we got such a good place. We had a Thermos of tea. We sat on the curb drinking tea and eating oatcakes. By the time the bands came, the crowd was so big you were just moved along with them. It was like the ocean. I was swept away by the crowd and I lost my grandfather."

"Were you scared?"

"Oh, no. It was the end of the war, dearie. Everyone was so *happy*."

"But *you* were lost."

"But I was found again," said Dorothy.

Dorothy reached across the table and picked the pie crust off Stephanie's plate.

"Are you finished with this?" she said. Not waiting for a reply, she finished it herself.

They waved down a cab to take them back to their hotel. It was dark. As they bumped along, Stephanie asked Dorothy about the years after the war.

"Everything was grey," she said.

She pulled a little package of cookies out of her purse. She held them out.

"Squashed fly biscuit?" she asked.

It was a soft cracker with raisins. Stephanie took a biscuit, and they ate quietly, and then Stephanie said, "You were telling me about after the war."

"We won," said Dorothy. "But you wouldn't think it. There was nothing to eat. We were on rations. We got one egg a month. One each. So two eggs. Mother used to put them on the mantel, and we would talk about how we were going to cook them.

"You had to line up for everything. If you saw a line, you would get in it and ask what you were lining up for afterwards. They would tell you, *tomatoes*, and you would wait for an hour, or maybe two, and when you got there they would give you two tomatoes."

Stephanie was peering out the window; they were going by Buckingham Palace. Dorothy didn't seem to notice.

Dorothy was saying, "*We* were better off than most. We used to get packages from my aunt Betty in Canada. Tins. Butter or meat. Once they sent eggs sealed in lard. But they had gone bad."

"You had an aunt in Canada?" said Stephanie.

"Cape Breton," said Dorothy.

"That's where my grandmother lives," said Stephanie, staring across the dark cab.

"Your grandmother *Margaret*," said Dorothy.

"How did you know?" said Stephanie.

"Because Margaret is my cousin," said Dorothy, as if this was the most obvious thing in the world. "Betty, who sent the food, was Margaret's mother. *Your* great-grandmother. *My* aunt."

Stephanie looked dumbstruck. "If your aunt was my great-grandmother—that means we *are* related."

Dorothy snorted.

"I mean closely," said Stephanie.

The taxi had pulled up in front of the hotel. Stephanie stood on the street while Dorothy paid the driver. Her head was spinning.

She *called* Dorothy her aunt, but she knew Dorothy wasn't *really* her aunt. She had known there was some connection, but she always thought it was distant and dubious. It had never dawned on her that she and Dorothy actually shared a past.

They went into the hotel but not to their room. As they stood in the lobby, Dorothy said, "I think we should have a whisky, don't you?"

The hotel bar was almost as small as their bedroom. Three tables, maybe four.

Stephanie said, "I can't believe you know Grandma."

"Of course I know Margaret. I got a letter from her last month. What are you thinking? Of course we are that closely related. You are my first cousin."

"I am?" said Stephanie.

"Twice removed," said Dorothy, waving at the barman for another whisky.

Dorothy leaned forward. She said, "I think we should drink these until we fall over."

Stephanie picked up her drink and started to say something. Her voice cracked. She took a sip and tried again.

"What did you mean when you said everything was grey?"

"Oh yes," said Dorothy. "I was going to tell you how grey everything was. Mother used to wash my clothes in the sink and it used to turn the water black."

Stephanie frowned.

"It was the coal dust, dearie," said Dorothy. "It was everywhere. Even your underwear made the water black.

"Didn't they ever tell you about the fogs?"

Stephanie shook her head, no. No one had told her about the fogs. Dorothy sighed. She said, "I have to do everything in this family."

"It was 1952," said Dorothy. "The coldest winter we had ever had. I was a little younger than you are today. We had to wear our coats and hats in class. The men in the offices sat all day in their coats too. You never took off your coat. At night my mother and I would sit around the gas fire in our clothes with a wool dressing gown over our clothes, and a scarf, and a hat. One night the water froze in our toilet bowl.

"What was I talking about?"

"The fog," said Stephanie.

"Oh," said Dorothy, "yes. It came at night. It was so thick. I remember one night Ellen Macdonald came for supper, and when it was time for her to go, and my mother opened the door and Ellen stepped outside, she was completely swallowed by it. She just took one step, and she disappeared. You have no idea. You have never seen anything like it. I was afraid Ellen wouldn't be able to find her way home.

"It lasted four days. Later we learned it was from all the coal fires, and it was very toxic. But we didn't know then. And people were so cold they kept burning their fires. No one knew. And then people started to die. That's how Charles died."

"My *great*-grandfather," said Stephanie.

"Great-*great*-grandfather," said Dorothy. "He went to the hospital. He had to walk because you couldn't see to drive. If you were driving, you had to have someone walking in front of you. The hospitals were full. They sent him home again. He turned blue. It's true," said Dorothy, "I was your age. I saw it."

"You were my age," said Stephanie quietly. She was looking at Dorothy, but she was talking to herself.

Stephanie flew home two days later. She sat in a window seat with a porcelain hedgehog in her lap. That night in the hotel bar, she'd asked Dorothy to put her name on the entire hedgehog collection. Dorothy had made her take one home.

Stephanie stared out the window during the entire flight. She didn't watch the movie or say a word to the man in the seat beside her. An uncommon melancholy had settled upon her, like a sorrow from long ago. It was the oddest feeling. As if there was something she was supposed to remember.

About four hours into the flight, the pilot announced they were flying over Cape Breton. Stephanie was full of questions. Where would she be today if her great-grandmother hadn't gone to Cape Breton? What if she had gone to Australia instead? Or South Africa? And Charles, who had turned blue and died of fog. She wished she could meet Charles. She felt if they could meet in the little bar in Durrants Hotel, he would tell her something important.

She had never thought about the web of influences spun around her, the long line of connective tissue. The bigness of it all diminished her and filled her with a sense of wonder all at once. For the first time, she felt a connection and responsibility to other generations. Those who had been. Those yet coming.

When the plane touched down, she handed her hedgehog to the man in the seat beside her. As they taxied toward the terminal, she pulled her sweater off and wrapped it carefully around the hedgehog and then gently tucked it into her knapsack.

"It's very old," she said to the man beside her. "It used to belong to my great-aunt. Three times removed."

Dear Mr. McLean,

My husband and I are having a tremendous blow-up right now, and we've decided that we need an arbitrator to sort things out. We were looking for someone with a keen critical ability, sound judgment and true wisdom. Unfortunately, we have not been able to find anyone like that. The other day, listening to your show on the radio, my husband piped up and said, "What about Stuart McLean? He seems like a guy with time on his hands."

So, we are coming to you with this question: When our time comes, should we be cremated or have a traditional burial?

Awaiting your response,
Emily

Dear Emily,

Personally, I have no intention of passing away, so I haven't given the matter of burials much thought. My friend Dave, however, has. Here's his story.

DAVE'S FUNERAL

Billy London called Dave at lunchtime. Any other Monday Dave might have missed his call, but not this Monday. This was a Monday in the middle of February, and it had been snowing all day. No one had been in his store for a couple of hours, because no one was out. And who could blame them? Dave wasn't about to go out either.

When Billy phoned, Dave was sitting in the comfy red chair by the cash register, his feet propped on a milk crate, a cup of soup balanced on the arm of the chair. He was multi-tasking, reading a music magazine from LA and listening to a new vinyl album—a tribute to Gordon Lightfoot and Neil Young recorded by a couple of young bands.

When the phone rang he scooped it up and said, "Just a minute." He reached over to the turntable and flipped up the tone arm; then he picked up the phone again.

"Billy?" he said. "Long time. What's up?"

Billy got right to the point. He said, "Aunt Ginger died, on the weekend. You're the only guy I could think of phoning. I thought you'd want to know."

Dave said, "Huh."

Billy said, "Yeah."

Then neither of them said anything.

It was Dave who broke the silence. "Did she make it? She must have made it."

Billy said, "No. She missed by four months. Three and a half, actually. Funeral's on Thursday. I thought you'd want to know. I already said that, didn't I?"

Aunt Ginger wasn't Billy's real aunt. She was a family friend of some sort. She had a house in Rosedale, and lived there alone. When Billy slipped over the border at Niagara Falls in 1968, dressed like a priest, she invited Billy to stay with her. He moved in for the better part of seven years. Or he kept his stuff there anyway. Billy played sax and was on the road all the time.

That didn't bother Aunt Ginger one bit. She was a piece of business—as tough as nails, and determined to live to be a hundred. She missed by three and a half months.

"Ninety-nine and three-quarters," said Billy. "It would have killed her to know that."

"How'd she die?" said Dave.

"Skiing accident," said Billy.

"Skiing?" said Dave.

"Well, snowboarding, actually," said Billy. "If you are going to be technical."

Billy and Dave sat together at the funeral, which turned out to be an altogether extraordinary affair.

It was organized by Aunt Ginger's only living relative—her older sister, Muriel. Muriel sat in a wheelchair at the front of the chapel as stiff as a plank. The two sisters hadn't spoken in twenty years.

It was Muriel who chose the reading: Raymond Chandler; Muriel who chose the decorations: balloons; and Muriel who chose the music. Muriel, who knew nothing whatsoever about music didn't know what to say when the funeral director asked her what they should play, so she asked what most people did. The funeral director said most people chose a classical piece. Muriel named the only classical piece she knew: "Flight of the Bumblebee."

When the music began, everybody in the congregation looked horrified—except Billy and Dave.

"Not bad, actually," whispered Dave to Billy, as the piece picked up speed.

"Perfect, actually," said Billy, nodding. "In so many ways."

The funeral was so awkward and wonderfully inappropriate that Dave couldn't stop talking about it for days.

"I want Zeppelin at my funeral," said Brian. Brian is a philosophy and calculus major who works part-time at the Vinyl Cafe.

"'Stairway to Heaven'?" said Dave. "It's eight minutes long. And totally obvious."

"Exactly," said Brian. What about you?"

"Never thought of it," said Dave. "I don't know. Uh. Don McLean. 'American Pie.'"

"'The day the music died'?" said Brian. "Talk about obvious. I hate that song."

"I was kidding," said Dave. "Wait a minute. Wait a minute. How about ... uh ... how about ... Kurt Weill. 'Mack the Knife'?"

"That's about a serial killer," said Brian.

"Right," said Dave. "That's not going to work. I can't believe I never thought about this before."

Dave was pulling on a sweatshirt. He was heading to Woodsworth's Books, barely a block away. He didn't need a coat.

"I'll be right back," he said.

"How about Cat Stevens?" called Brian. "Cat Stevens's 'Oh Very Young.'"

"Cat Stevens?" said Dave. He had his hand on the door handle. "I'd rather *die* than have Cat Stevens at my funeral."

"Hi," said Dave as he wandered into Dorothy's bookstore.

Dorothy was wearing her hair up. She was reading Gore Vidal.

"Hi," said Dorothy, smiling and putting her book down.

Dave picked up a leather bookmark from a box on the counter and started fiddling with it. "Listen," he said, "if I died tomorrow, and you were planning my funeral, what music would you choose? For my funeral."

Dorothy said, "Oh, no. What is it this time?"

"No. No," said Dave. "I'm fine. I'm fine. This is hypothetical."

"Hypothetically fine?" said Dorothy. "Or hypothetically dying?"

"Come on," said Dave. "I'm serious."

"If you were to die and I was planning your funeral?"

"I said that," said Dave. "The music."

"Cat Stevens," said Dorothy.

"Brian phoned you," said Dave. "You've been talking to Brian."

Two minutes later Dave walked into his friend Kenny Wong's café. Wong's Scottish Meat Pies.

Kenny was sitting at his cluttered desk, in the middle of the restaurant. He looked up when Dave came in. "Hey," he said. "Dorothy called. I'm just working on my list."

He leaned over his desk and pushed a piece of paper along the countertop. "So far I have 'The Chicken Dance' and 'The Beer Barrel Polka.'"

Morley was standing in front of the stove, working on a big pot of chili.

"It's for the wake," she said when Dave walked in the back door. "I have it all worked out. We are going to play 'dead teen' songs. 'Leader of the Pack.' 'Last Kiss.' And 'Tell Laura I Love Her.' Unless, of course, you die in a snowstorm looking for a lost horse. Then we'll play the one by Michael Murphy."

"'Wildfire,'" said Dave. "Who called?"

"Everyone," said Morley.

Later that night, as they were lying in bed, Dave dropped his book on the floor, pushed himself up on an elbow and said, "Can I ask you something? Seriously."

Morley was reading a design magazine. She rested the magazine on her chest. Dave said, "If *you* died ... what am I supposed to do? Do you want to be buried? Or what?"

Morley said, "Cremated. After that I don't care. Put me out with the recycling."

"I'm serious," said Dave.

Morley turned her head and looked at him. "Me too," she

said. She picked up her magazine. "I love this magazine," she said.

Dave dropped in on Dorothy the next morning, before he opened his store.

"If I was going to be truthful," he said to Dorothy, "if I was going to be perfectly and totally honest, I want to be buried with a flashlight and a cellphone."

"Just in case?" said Dorothy.

"Well … it happens," said Dave. Then, into the silence, the two of them staring at each other, he added two small words: "Or frozen."

"Just in case," said Dorothy.

"Exactly," said Dave.

Dave went to Kenny's for lunch. He sat on his usual stool, at the end of the counter, by Kenny's desk.

"If I die—" said Dave, chasing a snow pea around his plate with his chopsticks.

"*When* you die," said Kenny.

"Whatever," said Dave. "*If* I die. *When* I die. What's the difference?"

"Acceptance," said Kenny.

Dave was in a state, no doubt about it. And the state, as states tend to, was intensifying. He was talking to pretty much everyone about this. On the weekend he even talked to Mary Turlington. Or more to the point, Mary talked to him. They bumped into each other in the grocery store, by the yoghurt.

Dave was standing in front of the dairy cooler, feeling

overwhelmed, when Mary breezed in and began plucking up containers of yoghurt.

"Lactose free, 2 percent," said Mary without even saying hello.

"Thanks," said Dave, squinting at the tub she handed him. How could she possibly know more about his family's fridge than he did?

Mary changed gears. "I made our arrangements years ago," she said.

Dave was looking for more of the lactose-free yoghurt.

Mary said, "Over there." Then she said, "You know the three most important things about burial."

Dave stared at her, blankly.

Mary said, "Location, location, location." Then she said, "Do you have any idea how hard it is to find a prime gravesite?"

"Prime?" said Dave. Okay, he had forgotten about the yoghurt.

"Mature trees. Good landscaping. I looked for months. It's like buying a second property."

Mary was piling a staggering selection of yoghurt into her cart, plucking the containers off the shelf like she was picking apples.

"Bert had his heart set on a cottage. But I ran the numbers ... a plot is a far better investment. Do you want me to hook you up with my funeral director?"

Dave looked horrified. "No," he said. "No. No. No."

He was holding his hands in front of his chest and actually backing away from her.

Mary took a hard look at him and shook her head.

"It's coming," she said. "You can't stop it. And you shouldn't fear it. It's simple biology. Something we all should come to terms with."

Dave eats lunch at Kenny's café a couple of days a week.

"*If* I die," said Dave one lunchtime, "I always thought it would be nice to be buried, somewhere, maybe … I don't know. I haven't thought about this a lot. But somewhere with trees and squirrels maybe, or maybe a rabbit or something. So it would be nice, you know, for people who visit. A nice place. With animals."

"Uh-huh," said Kenny. Kenny was at his desk, working on a camera with a small screwdriver.

Kenny didn't look up. He said, "Like a petting zoo."

"Not like the goldfish," said Dave.

"What?" said Kenny.

Kenny put down the screwdriver and looked at Dave for the first time.

"Morley is going to have me cremated and then she is going to flush me down the toilet. Like the goldfish."

Kenny said, "You had the goldfish cremated?"

Mary left a message on the record-store phone. A name. And a phone number. And that's how Dave ended up, sitting, like a supplicant, across the large mahogany desk belonging to Mr. Lionel Gallop—owner, director and sole employee of the Sunshine Funeral Home.

"There is much to consider," said Mr. Gallop. "Choices *must* be made. And if *you* don't make them, someone *else* will."

It was as if he knew about Aunt Ginger and "The Flight of the Bumblebee."

Then Mr. Gallop leaned forward and lowered his voice.

"It's not unusual," he said, "to find boxes of ashes stacked on funeral parlour shelves. Boxes that are never collected."

He took Dave to see the cemetery a week later. Dave pointed to a treed knoll in a shady corner.

"There, maybe?" said Dave.

Mr. Gallop laughed. "Oh we couldn't afford *that*, I'm afraid."

He took Dave's elbow and steered him away from the little knoll. They walked along the path without saying anything, past a stand of leafy maples, around some flower beds, until they came to a stretch of hard, dusty grass that looked like an abandoned playground. Mr. Gallop smiled and held his arm out.

"Maybe here," he said.

With each passing minute Dave was becoming more and more certain he would be spending eternity on a shelf of the Sunshine Funeral Home. Until, of course, the shelf was full, and Mr. Gallop had to make room for others.

"Are there really," said Dave, "uhh ..."

"Uncollected?" said Mr. Gallop. "Yes. That does happen. We hold them for as long as we can. After twenty-five years we give them to the city."

"To the *city*?" said Dave.

"They're put in a common grave." Mr. Gallop was holding his hands in front of him. "But with the utmost dignity."

He looked sad. Prayerful. Lost in thought.

Dave stood beside him, waiting.

After a moment Mr. Gallop turned abruptly and smiled. "Hopefully," he said, "if you make good choices, if you make the *right* choices, in the years that come, you will be able to … *rest in peace*."

He nodded his head and made a little mewing sound.

"Mmm?"

And so, Dave bought a coffin. He had to do something. He didn't see any plots he liked, and he had to act. He had to make a choice.

The coffin was not altogether a bad decision. It was neither the most expensive nor the cheapest. It was pine, but *red* pine—a coffin that seemed to fit his station in the world.

"A good choice," said Mr. Gallop. "A reasonable beginning."

Mr. Gallop shook Dave's hand and gave him a booklet with a list of things that he should think about.

"There's so much to decide," said Mr. Gallop, his arm on Dave's shoulder. "Flowers. The, uh, venue. Music."

"That's how this all began," said Dave.

"The memorial," said Mr. Gallop, oblivious. "Epitaph, printed materials for the booklets, slides, collages." He waved his hand in the air. "The outfit—for the deceased."

"That's me," said Dave.

"Announcements," said Mr. Gallop, nodding. "And, of course, the eulogy."

"The eulogy?" said Dave.

"It's much, much more than a way of saying farewell," said Mr. Gallop. "If it's done with the right touch, it can bring the person to life. Uh. In the minds of the beloved."

Dave began his eulogy the next day at lunch. He got a pad of lined paper and worked on it at the kitchen table.

He wrote his name at the top of the page. Centred. Then he skipped a line and wrote: *He is*.... He stared at the words; then he crumpled the paper and threw it at the garbage.

He missed.

He took another piece of paper and wrote his name at the top again. This time, under it, he wrote: *He was*....

He stared at that. It seemed like tempting the fates. He crumpled the second page and threw it at the garbage.

He is.... *He* was.... Someone else could change the tense.

He was ... one of the most—*Dave's pen hovered*—one of the most.... He crumpled that page and bounced it off the rim of the garbage. He started again.

Born in the village of Big Narrows, son of Charlie and Margaret and one of the most ... one of the most ... *Forgiving? Generous? Remarkable? Humble?* ... humble.

He was just finishing up the first page when the doorbell rang. Two guys in blue coveralls were standing on the stoop. They looked like roofers. The bigger guy did the talking.

"We got your coffin," said the bigger guy.

There had been some sort of misunderstanding.

"There's been a misunderstanding," said Dave.

"Where do you want your coffin?" said the big guy.

It hadn't occurred to Dave he would be taking *delivery* of the coffin.

"Who did you *think* was going to get it?" said the big guy.

Dave had them put the coffin in the garage. He covered it with blankets. Thank God no one was home.

In his rush to hide his final resting place, Dave had left his eulogy on the kitchen table. By the time he remembered it, he was back at work, and Stephanie, home for study week, was reading it in disbelief.

"Who wrote this crud?" she said at supper, waving the eulogy in the air. "They obviously never *met* you."

"It's nothing," said Dave.

He managed to get the coffin to the record store before anyone saw it.

There is a room over the store where Dave keeps stuff— souvenirs mostly, paper from the days when he worked in the concert business. There are handwritten set lists, notes, letters, snapshots and some stage clothes. All manner of stuff. It's an amazing collection of memorabilia, assembled partly for sentimental reasons, but mostly because Dave could never bear to throw anything out. It never occurred to him while he was squirrelling the stuff away that it would be valuable one day.

It is how he augments his living. He trades and sells pieces when he needs serious money, or if someone desperately wants something.

He figured he could keep the coffin upstairs with his collection until he figured out what to do with it.

But you try getting a coffin up a flight of stairs by yourself. And tell me who you would call to help if you didn't want to be explaining yourself for the next six months. So Dave humped his coffin to the back of his store, covered it with blankets and put some crates of records on top of it.

And then one rainy afternoon in March, in the middle of a week of rainy afternoons, a week when no one had been in the store all day, Dave found himself looking at the blanket-covered coffin wondering what it would be like to be inside.

Not many people wonder about things like that.

Fewer have an opportunity to find out.

Once the thought had entered Dave's mind, he couldn't shake it.

The store had been pretty much empty all week.

He had way too much time on his hands.

He removed the milk crates of records and piled them on the floor. He ran his hand over the shiny coffin. It was actually a beautiful piece of craftsmanship. A pine box to be sure, but a pine box with the lustre of ebony.

He was about to climb in—just for a second, just to see—when it occurred to him that it would hardly be an accurate experience, lying there in his comfy sweater and cords. Surely, when he was laid out, it would be a more formal thing. He went upstairs. There was a jacket up there that once belonged to Eric Clapton. There was, in fact, a whole rack of clothing. A shirt Frank Sinatra Jr. had left in a dressing room in the Poconos. A tie that had once belonged to Paul Anka. He slipped off his sweater and put on the shirt, the tie and Eric's jacket.

And then he spotted Alice Cooper's makeup kit.

A job worth doing, as his father-in-law, Roy, used to say, is worth doing properly.

He powdered his face. He looked in the mirror. He looked great—which is to say, he looked dead.

He went downstairs. He ran back upstairs, grabbed some candles and then ran back downstairs.

He lifted the lid of the coffin and propped it up, checking

the hinge to make sure it wouldn't slam shut. He lit the candles. He dimmed the lights. He put on some music. Etta James. "At Last."

Then he crawled into the box. Tumbled into it actually, bum first.

There was not as much room in there as you might think. He had to squirm around awkwardly to arrange himself. In fact, it was cramped. But the silk lining was smooth and soft, and there was a nice layer of padding between him and the bottom of the casket.

Not bad, thought Dave. *Quite comfortable, actually. Peaceful even.* Dave folded his arms over his chest. He closed his eyes.

He wasn't *sound* asleep, but he wasn't wide awake either. He was somewhere in that foggy world between dreams and thought, lying in his coffin, the candles flickering at each of the corners, trying to get in touch with eternity, when the front door opened, and someone walked into the record store.

Dave thought he had locked the door. He was sure he had locked the door.

"Hello," said a voice.

Apparently he had not.

He didn't move a muscle.

"Hello," called the voice again.

It was a woman's voice. And it sounded familiar.

"David," it said, "are you here?"

It almost sounded like Mary Turlington.

That was ridiculous. Mary Turlington had *never* been in Dave's store. Uptight and sanctimonious Mary Turlington wasn't interested in anything "used." Mary was suspicious of used goods. She preferred reproductions to antiques.

But that very morning Mary had received a letter informing her that there was room opening up at the graveyard where she had bought her plot. It hadn't occurred to her to wonder exactly *how* room would *open up* at a cemetery. The only thing that mattered was that Dave had an overly dramatic approach to death and he had to get over it.

Mary was on a mission. She had dragged herself to the store for Morley's sake. She was going to help this silly man grow up and accept his mortality. She was going to get him organized. Death was just another aspect of the housekeeping of life. You pay your bills, you buy groceries, you mow the lawn—and you make your funeral arrangements.

She actually hadn't meant to go in, however.

Damn, she thought as she went through the door, *I was going to call him.*

It smelled funny in there—like incense. Or worse. There was suspicious music playing. The type of music that people play when they are up to no good. And it was dark.

The place was giving her the creeps.

"David," she called. Where was he? And what did he do in this dusty, dark shop all day—by himself?

"David? Are you here?"

Mary hesitated by the door and then stepped in. What could he be doing back there that he couldn't do out in the open?

She caught sight of the candles.

Just the sort of childish display she would expect of Dave. Against her better judgment, she kept going.

Dave was lying stiffly in the coffin. He was thinking that if he were very quiet, if he didn't move a muscle, Mary would assume that the shop was empty. And leave.

Blessed mother of Jesus. Her footsteps were getting closer and closer.

Then they stopped abruptly.

As Mary moved further into the store, her eyes adjusted to the gloom.

"Blessed mother of Jesus," said Mary. It wasn't a mannequin in the coffin. It was a body.

Ohmigod, thought Dave.

"Ohmigod," said Mary.

Every nerve ending in Mary's brain told her to get out of there. And to get out of there fast. But she couldn't help herself. She was drawn toward the casket.

Don't move, thought Dave. *Don't move a muscle.*

He lay there for an eternity.

But eventually he couldn't help himself.

Very slowly and very carefully, Dave opened one eye.

Unfortunately it was the eye Mary happened to be staring at.

Maybe if she had recognized Dave things would have worked out differently. But she didn't recognize Dave. It was dark in there, and he was made up. And he was wearing a tie, for heaven's sake.

So Mary stumbled back, her heart pounding, watching as the body rose up and struggled clumsily out of the casket like a zombie in a horror movie.

Then the body said, "Hello, Mary."

This is how it ends? thought Mary. *Zombies?*

Then she hit the ground.

The letter from Stephanie arrived the following week.

Dear Dad,

Dave got it at lunchtime. He showed it to Morley after supper.

"Did you tell her to write this?" asked Dave.

"No," said Morley. "I didn't."

Dear Dad,

Mom told me you have been worried about dying.

She told me that's why you were writing your eulogy. I want to apologize for making fun of you. I am sorry I laughed at you. I am sorry I made fun of it.

When Paula's dad died, she had to talk at his funeral. I started wondering what I would say if I had to talk at yours.

I decided I would tell people about the eye patch. Do you remember that? I think I was about six. I don't even remember why I had to wear that stupid patch. All I remember is that Dr. Milne said I had to wear an eye patch and that I refused. Nothing was going to make me wear that patch. I cried all the way home from the doctor's office. When we got into the house, you sat me down at the kitchen table.

You pulled out two eye patches, and you put the first one over your own eye. You said we would have a deal. You said that I would wear my patch until Dr. Milne told me I could take it off. And you would wear yours until I told you to take it off. I said, "But people are going to look at you funny." And you said, "Well, if they do, I guess I can talk to you about it. You might know how that feels." Do you remember how we decorated them? I think you drew flowers on mine. I don't remember. But I remember I drew a huge, gross, red eye on yours. And you wore it for a whole week before I let you take it off. You wore it to work, and when you took the car to the garage, and out to dinner at the Turlingtons'. I can't believe I made you do that.

If I had to talk at your funeral, I would tell people the story about the eye patch. Then I would tell them that's the kind of dad you were. That you would do anything for me and Sam. Even if it made you look silly.

I love you, Daddy.

Steph

P.S . I don't want you to die. If you die I am going to kill you.

Dave took Stephanie's letter to the store. It is still in the drawer by the cash. Sometimes when he reads it, it makes him happy. Sometimes it makes him cry.

Mary hasn't been back in the store, although she has been over for dinner. All in all, it was a successful evening.

Dave still has the coffin. It's still in the back of the store. But it is not covered anymore. There is a display of forty-fives in it: teenage death songs.

Dear Mr. McLean,

My father and I are planning to spend the summer weekends renovating our cottage, but it seems a shame that no one will be able to get up there during the week to continue the work. My dad pointed out that as your show is aired by a public broadcaster, we, as taxpayers, are essentially coughing up the dough for your salary. With that in mind, we were hoping that you could make yourself available for a few days this summer. I've enclosed directions to the cabin.

Jeff

Dear Jeff,

Well, when you put it that way, it is hard not to agree. However you might want to read the following story before we go ahead with this arrangement.

PETIT LAC NOIR

No one ever gasps in awe when they see the Laurentian Mountains for the first time. Rather than express awe, first-time visitors, who have spent a morning being toured through Les Laurentides, are more apt to turn to whoever has been driving them around and ask that mortifying question so many have asked before them, "When do we get to the mountains?"

The Laurentians *are*, admittedly, more hills than mountains. They roll, rather than tower, but they roll with a dignity that befits one of the oldest mountain ranges in the world. The Laurentians, and the pleasant lakes that dot the hills, make you feel that both comfort and constancy are to be had in this changing world.

Ahh. *Tous les lacs des Laurentides*: Lac Marois, Lac Saint-Amour, Lac des Seize Îles. *Et tous les* little lakeside villages: Saint-Sauveur, Saint-Rémi, Val des Bois and, of course, Notre-Dame des Plaines—hardly a village, really. One gas station, two general stores, a Catholic church and a handful of cottages.

Notre-Dame des Plaines and Petit Lac Noir. The little village, and the little lake lapping just over the hill, just behind the church, where Jean-François Clément and his family have

whiled away summer afternoons since, well, since Jean-
François was a boy. And before.

Every Friday at 5:30, precisely, Jean-François, a small-animal
vet, closes his office. If you were to arrive at say 5:35 and find
him in the parking lot, he would say, *Well, I would like to help
you, mais le bureau est fermé.* And he would give you, or
whoever it was standing there holding their sick cat or
limping dog, directions to the nearest emergency clinic.

He would, incidentally, mean it. Jean-François is nothing if
not both earnest and honest. He *would* like to help you. But
how could he? At 5:30 on a Friday? Five-thirty on a Friday is
when he picks up his wife, Marie-Josée, and they drive, like his
father did before him, to the cottage for the weekend. They
stop on the way of course, like his father did, at the *boulanger*
in Shawbridge to pick up a country loaf and a baguette.

The idea of phoning Marie-Josée and leaving later wouldn't
occur to Jean-François. Five-thirty is when you leave.

The cottage has been in Jean-François' family for five generations. For five generations, Cléments have been learning
lessons from the mountains. And what they have learned is to
pray at the altar of tradition.

The cottage has been passed down like a religious relic.
Nothing about it has changed. Not the way you get there, nor
the things you do when you arrive. It is a cathedral of
constancy, although you mustn't get the idea that it's run
down. It has been kept up perfectly. Though not up*dated.* It is
one of those endangered species. A cottage in the old style.

Well, there has been one change. After much heated discussion, and threats, and pressure from his mother—after a

crusade, you might say—Jean-François' father did install an indoor toilet; but he left the old outhouse standing, and whenever he was angry with his wife, he would revert to using it, grumbling out the kitchen door even in the middle of the night. So there is an indoor toilet. But there is also a woodstove and a summer kitchen. Five generations of believers. And Jean-François is a faithful member of the church.

Marie-Josée, who has hankered for a hot-water tank at the cottage, and maybe even a shower, has had problems with this. They have argued about this, Jean-François and his wife.

"*Ils sont tous morts. Tes parents, ton grand-papa,*" she has said. "*C'est à ton tour.*"

Jean-François will hear none of it. The Laurentians, you might say, suit him to a T.

To put it precisely, like the mountains, he is not a man who embraces change. For Jean-François, *Je me souviens*, the words on the licence plate of his Ford station wagon—the exact same car his father favoured—aren't a *political* statement. For Jean-François, *Je me souviens* is a way of life.

Every Friday at 5:30 precisely he and Marie-Josée drive north. And every summer, during the construction holiday at the end of July, they spend two weeks on the coast of Maine. Just like he did when he was a boy.

The ocean, as his father used to say, is something you can count on.

When he goes to Maine, Jean-François walks two miles along the beach every day. At eight in the morning and again at four in the afternoon—the hours when you won't get burned. He collects sea glass and driftwood. And he brings back one piece of each every summer. He began his collection when he was a boy. The sea glass goes on the windowsill. The driftwood lines the path to the lake. He appreciates the way the weather has worked the glass and the wood. He has no time for so-called artists who hack at a piece of wood to create a sculpture in just a few weeks. Or months.

Jean-François loves Maine.

Well, that's not totally true. He used to love it. Things have been changing in Maine. The old highway is getting busier. Franchise joints and condos are popping up everywhere. The truth is, he has grown tired of it lately, and these days the thing he loves most of all about Maine is the Saturday in August that he and Marie-Josée return to the cottage.

After all, is there anything more pleasant, or more reassuring, than an afternoon at Petit Lac Noir? Marie-Josée on the chaise longue, reading *Marie Claire* and sipping homemade lemonade; Jean-François trimming the front lawn. The lawn his great-grandfather planted and cared for— keeping it up is Jean-François' pride and joy.

That's how they spent the last Saturday of this August. Most of it, anyway. Jean-François puttering in the shed, Marie-Josée reading magazines, although after lunch Marie-Josée did set Jean-François to work in the garden, a huge bed of wildflowers that stretches right across the front of the cottage.

"I want it looking its very best," she said. "*Mais oui!* Remember who is coming."

They were expecting guests. A younger couple whom they befriended years ago and hadn't seen in ... could it be that long. *Ce n'est pas possible* ... a decade?

At five o'clock precisely, Jean-François came in, took off his gardening gloves and said, "*Eh ben.*"

Marie-Josée glanced at the clock over the kitchen door. It was time for his Saturday swim. Jean-François has a dip every Saturday at five—until the Saturday after Labour Day, when he folds his trunks and puts them away until St-Jean Baptiste.

She smiled at him and reached out and touched his face. The scars on his cheek were raised and a little inflamed.

It was hot. He had been working hard. She kissed him on the forehead and said, "*Je pense que je te joindrai.*"

The scars were one of the great lessons in Jean-François' life. He got them in an altercation with a deranged cockatoo.

For the first ten years of his practice, he didn't treat birds at his clinic. But after a protracted campaign waged by his receptionist, an impatient and flighty girl, he relented and agreed to treat the cockatoo, the first and last bird he ever admitted.

He had stayed late, as was his habit on a Tuesday night, Tuesday night being the night he does the books. So he was, as fate would have it, without backup when he went down to the basement to check the assorted dogs, cats, rodents and the solitary bird, which appeared to be going bald, losing feathers to some unknown malaise.

He was holding the cockatoo up to his face, and whispering to it in that ridiculous baby style that birds seem to encourage, thinking while he did that he might have been too inflexible about birds, that perhaps his receptionist had been right all along and he should consider apologizing, and wondering what he might possibly say to *her*, when the cockatoo abruptly turned and said something to *him* that sounded disturbingly adult. Something you would never hear in a church.

And then the bird sank his beak into Jean-François' cheek and wouldn't let go. Or perhaps couldn't.

Both Jean-François and the cockatoo panicked when they realized what had happened, and the two of them began flapping wildly, the bird shredding Jean-François' cheek with his claws. Until Jean-François realized panic wasn't going to get him anywhere, and he stumbled into the O.R., grabbed a needle that he had prepared for the next day's surgery and plunged it into the bird's back, anesthetizing it. Then he drove himself to Emergency at Hotel-Dieu with the drugged cockatoo dangling from his face like an earring.

This was over thirty years ago.

The intern who removed the bird still tells the story at dinner parties.

"I thought the guy was crazy," he will begin. "He was barely coherent. He was screaming, 'It's going to wake up. It's going to wake up.'

"I said, 'That parrot isn't going to wake up. That parrot is dead.'

"'No. No,' he said. 'It's just resting.'"

Over the years the doctor has embellished the story, of course.

"It was a huge parrot," he says, holding his hands about two feet apart. "And it was dangling from his cheek. At first I thought it was jewellery. But it was a parrot."

These days, in his version the bird does wake up halfway through the operation and there is a heroic struggle.

In fact, the bird slept through it all. In fact, even after he had removed it, the intern still believed the bird was stuffed, or dead, and he had put it down on a shelf, and he was stitching up Jean-François when the bird did wake. The rest is more or less true the way he tells it—he and Jean-François trapped in the triage with this crazed and angry cockatoo dive-bombing them, the three of them crashing about, and the large nurse from the Gaspé who burst in and grabbed the cockatoo right out of the air, like it was nothing more than a fly and snapped its neck.

Jean-François' wound got infected and healed poorly. And he learned his lesson. It wasn't a new one. More a confirmation than a lesson, really. But there you have it. Plain as day. Change never led to any good. From then on he stuck to dogs and cats. He went to the cottage on the weekends, and to Old Orchard Beach in Maine every July.

The scars slowly faded with the years, and these days only announce themselves when Jean-François is tired or upset. He does his best to avoid both.

Dave met Jean-François the summer after he and Morley were married. They met when Dave and Morley rented a cottage just down the road from the Cléments. That was the summer Dave and Morley had already spent what little vacation money they had on a trip to Holland. They had flown there for a weekend in February so Morley could fulfill one of her lifetime dreams and skate along the frozen canals.

Dave heard about it—the cottage down the road from the Cléments' place—from an old friend in Montreal.

"You'd love it there," he said. "No one will bother you, and it would be cheap."

This was, as I said, a summer when cheap was important.

His friend called back a week later. "You can have it for free," he said. "All you have to do is a few chores."

"Cool," said Dave.

They left at the beginning of August, in Morley's old orange and white Volkswagen van. The trip took almost ten hours. They went along old Highway 7, stopping every couple of hours—for coffee, for a swim; at a cheese factory outside of Perth; for cheeseburgers at a little stand in the middle of nowhere. They shared the driving, the way they shared just about everything in those days. They crossed the Ottawa River at Hawkesbury and from there rattled north onto Highway 329 and into the grey-blue Laurentians.

As they pulled in to Notre-Dame des Plaines, Van Morrison was cranked on the cassette deck, "Brown Eyed Girl," and Dave was pounding the steering wheel in time to the music. Morley was squinting at a piece of paper.

"Okay," she said, reaching out and turning the music down. "It says to make the following turns: *à gauche, à gauche, à droite.*"

Dave said, "Huh?"

Morley said, "That means left, left, right ... *right?*"

"Right," said Dave.

"Right," said Morley. "But not right away. *Gauche, gauche,* then right."

"Right," said Dave.

"But first left, left," said Morley.

"Then right ... right?" said Dave.

"Right," said Morley.

This went on for several minutes more than it should have, and they were feeling pretty goofy as they passed the gas station, and the general store, and the white church, and eventually pulled onto a dirt road with a bunch of cottages.

The road had two ruts down each side and a strip of grass down the middle. It was narrow enough that tree branches were brushing the side of the van. Dave slapped the steering wheel and cranked the music back up.

"This is going to be great," he said.

They passed a few cottages and then saw the lake for the first time and a small, neat cottage with pale blue trim.

"Well, that was easy," said Dave as he pulled in to the driveway.

Easy until they lifted the welcome mat and there was no key where the key was supposed to be. Morley stood there for a moment, looking around, and then she slid her hand under a planter on the step beside the mat. She smiled. *There* was the key.

The house was in much better shape than Dave had been led to believe. It was old, to be sure, but not rundown like his friend had warned. It was clean and neat and just about perfect.

"There's a wood stove," said Dave. "This is perfect."

Dave's friend had sent them a note explaining what they were expected to do in exchange for their free rent: take down the little wall between the kitchen and the living room and dig up the grass lawn so the owners could put in a garden.

"You think this is the wall they want down?" said Morley. She was pointing at the door between the kitchen and dining room.

Dave shrugged. They had a week. Time enough for work tomorrow.

"I'll get the bags," said Dave.

They found a bedroom and changed into their bathing suits. They headed across the lawn to the lake.

Morley said, "That's where they want the garden, I guess."

"Et voilà," said Dave.

They stood at the end of the dock gazing out at the lake. Then Morley touched him on the back and dove without testing the water. She dove clean and straight and flat. When she came up, her long hair was floating behind her. It was the first time Dave had seen her in water. The first time they had swum together.

She turned and flicked her hair and looked back. "It's beautiful," she said.

Dave stuck his foot in the lake and yanked it out.

"It's freezing," he said.

Tuesday they slept until ten, had a big breakfast on the porch, went swimming, ate lunch on the dock, read on the dock and napped on the dock. Morley was reading Alice Munro for the first time in her life. Dave was reading *Rolling Stone*.

After supper they went for a walk further down the road. All the way to the end where a little stream flowed into the lake.

They talked about each cottage they passed; some in good repair, a few neglected; one with a sagging moss-covered roof, one a brand-new A-frame that seemed glaringly out of place.

"I like ours the best," said Morley.

On Wednesday morning Morley made pancakes. They ate them on the porch. After they had cleaned up she said, "We should get to it."

Taking down a wood wall in an unfinished cottage shouldn't be too complicated. Dave began slowly and carefully, standing on a chair, gently prying the tongue-and-groove wallboards free with a hammer. By late afternoon, covered in sweat, his patience spent, he was stripped to the waist, ripping down the wall with a crowbar he had found in the woodshed.

While Dave attacked the wall, Morley was working on the garden.

"How big do you think they want it?" she asked.

Morley, still in her twenties, had never done any gardening in her life. She considered the lawn for a while and then marked out a rectangular bed that ran along the front of the house. She wasn't surprised that they wanted the grass out. It was so incongruous: The cottage had a woodsy feel to it; the lawn was as manicured as a putting green, flat, spongy and soft. Morley used an axe to hack out large chunks of grass. Then she pried the sod loose and stacked it at the end of the driveway.

Morley was finished in a couple of hours. She put the axe down and went inside and made lunch.

They ate on the dock again. When they had cleaned up, Morley stared at her garden and decided it wasn't big enough. She got the axe and ripped up another section of lawn. By supper, she had pulled up about a third of the grass.

"What do you think?" she said.

Dave thought she had made the garden way too big. He didn't say that, however.

"Good," he said. "It's good. It looks great."

Things were not looking great inside.

Halfway through the afternoon, Dave had uncovered a brick chimney. He had found a sledgehammer in the shed, and he had been going at the chimney for over two hours. It looked as if someone had lobbed a small explosive into the kitchen.

"This wasn't the way it was described to me," muttered Dave at eight on Friday morning.

They had been up since seven. For the second day running, Morley had set an alarm. They were leaving the next day. It was only eight and Dave was already sweating and covered in the brick dust which hung in the air of the cottage like smoke. But he was getting close. With any luck the chimney would be down by noon.

This was the day they met Jean-François and Marie-Josée.

As Dave and Morley hammered away at the kitchen, Jean-François and Marie-Josée were driving back from their two weeks in Maine.

As usual they were coming directly to their cottage to spend the last two weeks of their vacation at the lake. As they rolled up the autoroute, and the blue Laurentian Mountains rose up in front of them, Jean-François was having the same conversation they have every year. Mostly with himself.

"Well, that was nice," he said.

Marie-Josée nodded, unconvincingly.

"But," he added, "it's good to be home."

As they crested the big hill and began their descent into Notre-Dame des Plaines, Marie-Josée was staring out the car window, feeling a little desperate. They were going to spend the rest of the month at the lake, the exact same month she had lived through every year. She knew exactly how it was going to go.

On Monday mornings Jean-François would mow the lawn.

"The dandelions are terrible this year," he would say.

On Tuesdays, they would drive into Saint-Sauveur for groceries. Wednesdays was laundry. Thursdays they would barbecue. On Fridays, take a bike ride along the old Loken Trail.

At 2:30 each afternoon, they would swim. At nine o'clock Jean-François would pour their final glass of wine. At eleven o'clock, lights out. It was like summer camp, except there wouldn't be one solitary surprise. Not one unexpected moment.

I should get him a whistle, she thought.

"*Pardon?*" said Jean-François.

When he turned the station wagon into their driveway, Marie-Josée blinked. She stared at the house and then at her husband.

Jean-François had gone completely slack-jawed.

There was an orange and white Volkswagen van parked in their normal spot. There was a pile of rubble beside the van.

And as they sat there, a guy stood up from Marie-Josée's chaise longue and walked toward them. The guy was grinning from ear to ear.

Jean-François opened his car door, got out and stood there in an uncomprehending haze. And that was when he noticed their entire front lawn had been dug up. Well, okay, a third of it.

He staggered backwards, reaching out for the door of his car for support. He felt as if he were in a dream. He reached absentmindedly for his face and fingered his cheek. His scar was starting to throb. He managed to choke out a few words.

He said, "*Ça ça fait là là?*"

He was pointing at the disaster in front of him.

The guy who had been sitting in the chaise longue smiled, and bobbed his head encouragingly, and spoke the words he had been practising all week.

"*Bonjour,*" he said. "*Je m'appelle Dave.*"

Jean-François didn't actually faint. He did however sink to his knees, staring, in disbelief, at the pile of rubble and the ruined lawn—the lawn he had been weeding and spraying and mowing since he was tall enough to grasp the handle of the lawn mower. His pride and his joy.

Dave was still beaming at him as he went down. Dave thought he was joking. His kind of guy. So Dave went to his knees too. And they kneeled in front of each other for one long, silent uncomprehending moment.

Then Dave, who was thinking how happy the guy must be, reached out and grabbed Jean-François' hand and shook it. Then he put his arm around the older man's shoulders and led him into the kitchen, pointing proudly to where the kitchen wall used to be. The kitchen wall that Jean-François had stared at all his boyhood years.

Jean-François gasped in horror.

It suddenly occurred to him the guy might be a wing nut, maybe even dangerous. He tried to wrestle himself free. Where was Marie-Josée?

Marie-Josée was outside.

She had got out of the car and surveyed the piles of ripped sod, the scar of dirt across her lawn, and Marie-Josée had smiled.

"Well," she said, to no one in particular, "what I think we need is wildflowers."

Then she saw Morley standing uncertainly by the dock, and she pointed at the black earth and said, "I love what you've done with the place. Who are you, anyway?"

Morley said, "We're the renters."

And Marie-Josée said, "What renters?"

Which is when Jean-François burst out the front door, and Morley burst into tears.

It was Marie-Josée who settled everyone down. Once she managed that, it didn't take them long to work out what had happened.

Left, left, right ... right?

There had been one too many rights. Dave and Morley were supposed to be at the little cottage down the road, the one with the sagging, moss-covered roof.

They tried to clear out. It was Marie-Josée who insisted that they stay for dinner. While Marie-Josée prepared supper, Jean-François kept walking into the kitchen and staring dumbly at the place where the wall used to be.

From the kitchen he would walk to the lake, where he stood on the dock as the wind died and the sun settled. Something about all this felt familiar. Whatever it was, it was trying to bubble to the surface, but it just wouldn't come.

He went back to the house for the third time.

Marie-Josée was making a salad. Talking a mile a minute to this young English couple. They didn't seem so bad.

"*Ouvre le radio, mon oiseau; j'ai besoin de musique.*"

He wandered over to his father's old radio and absent-mindedly flicked it on. Then he stared at it. The radio. His father's old wooden radio.

"What?" said Marie-Josée.

"*Rien,*" said Jean-François. "Nothing."

But it was clear by the way he was staring at the radio it wasn't nothing at all. It was something, that's for sure.

Jean-François was remembering his first year as a vet. He had bought his father a new radio for his birthday—a portable Grundig transistor that he could take down to the dock. Jean-François was excited to give it to him. It was the first expensive thing he had ever bought his father.

His father didn't even pretend to be impressed. "It doesn't have tubes," he said. "It looks like a toy."

He didn't seem to care that *no tubes* was the point of it. Or that it was the best portable radio money could buy. That it was *supposed* to be small. He thought it looked flimsy.

"It is made of *plastic*," he said.

His father's old radio had a *wood* case. At first Jean-François was angry and hurt. How could his father be so dismissive of such a thoughtful gift? Why did his father reject everything that was different? Why couldn't his father move forward with the rest of the world?

Then one night, he watched his father pick up the little transistor radio. The old man squinted at the dials and fiddled with the antennae. Then he put it down and moved over to his big tube radio with its impressive mahogany floor stand. His father ran his hand lovingly over the wooden cabinet, and as he did, he looked suddenly old, and sad, and even a little afraid. And Jean-François understood.

It's unnerving to think you've figured out the world only to see it move on ahead of you, to find that the things that bring you comfort are obsolete, vanishing. To know that all of the signposts and symbols, all the information and skills you had spent your life mastering might be of no help to you in the future. Jean-François understood why his father might prefer the old and familiar to the new and sleek. The next time Jean-François visited, he packed the transistor radio into his suitcase and took it back to his apartment. It was still there in his basement workroom. The following Christmas he gave his father a set of fishing lures. But it saddened him that his father had *chosen* to be left behind. It frustrated him that his father couldn't see that the future was fresh and exciting, bursting with possibilities for anyone who embraced them.

The very first thing that he and Marie-Josée bought when they first married was a tiny colour-television set. Jean-François had been so proud of it, and of himself for getting it. That seemed long ago now, and while Jean-François liked to embrace all the new technology that came his way, standing on the porch staring at the lake, it occurred to him that he had become more like his father than his twenty-year-old self would have thought possible.

He was on the porch, still staring at the lake, when a young man and woman glided by in a canoe.

"Eh ben," he said suddenly. "*Ça fait rien.*"

What he was trying to say was, *I like it.*

They ate outside in the screened-in part of the porch. They opened a bottle of wine. By the end of the second bottle, they were laughing, and they moved right past it, and beyond it, and every time they circled back to it, it seemed even funnier.

As they worked on dessert, Marie-Josée showed them her newest piece of blown glass, a piece that she had picked up in Maine.

It was a mobile—a clatter of little glass birds.

"*Les petits oiseaux de Marie-Josée*," said Jean-François, rolling his eyes. "Ha-ha-ha."

It turned out she called him *Monsier Oiseau.* The birdman.

For his fiftieth birthday, she had given him an antique birdcage with a stuffed parrot. It was hanging by their bed in the city.

"Where I *have* to look at it," said Jean-François, desperately.

It was clear that his feelings for the stuffed bird were complicated by love. He hated the bird. But he loved her; you could see that. And he loved that she had given it to him.

They stayed up too late. They drank too much wine.

Dave and Morley ended up staying overnight. And visiting each year for a couple of summers. This August was the first time they had seen Jean-François and Marie-Josée for over a decade.

When they saw each other, Dave and Jean-François both dropped to their knees, just like they did that afternoon a quarter of a century ago. It's a thing they do.

Then they got up (Dave had to help Jean-François, who uses a cane these days), and they walked down to the dock together, past the wildflowers that Marie-Josée put in.

There is no lawn left anymore—it is all wild and grassy now. So Dave and Jean-François walked along the path that goes through the tall, wavy grass. Dave trailed his hands through the lacy seedpods and said it looked very nice.

"I like it better," he said, "than it used to be. Than the lawn."

Then he tried in French.

He said, "*C'est plus sauvage.*"

"*Oui,*" said Jean-François. "*Plus* wild." Then he put his arm around Dave. "*Comme les montagnes,*" he said.

"*Oui,*" said Dave. "Wild *comme les montagnes.*"

Dear Stuart,

I have listened to your show for years, and you strike me as one of those people who has an opinion on just about everything. What do you have to say about this?

When I drive around a right-hand corner over thirty kilometres an hour, I hear a strange knocking coming from my trunk. I got my friend Bruce to ride in the trunk the other day to try to check exactly where it is coming from, but he couldn't tell. And then I pulled in to a Tim's parking lot and turned the engine off and had a smoke and thought I could still hear it, but that turned out just to be Bruce.

What do you think that might be? Do you think it is serious?

Yours sincerely,
Evan

Dear Evan,

Strange noises coming from a trunk are not something that should be ignored. Putting your friend back there was a good idea. But if he was unable to help, you might try some different approaches. Do you have a dog? You would be amazed what a good hunting dog will turn up in a trunk. You seem like a sensible fellow and I don't think I have to mention this, but under no circumstance should you venture in there yourself. I have attached a cautionary tale.

RAT-A-TAT-TAT

Dave was at Kenny Wong's café. He was sitting at the counter, eating a bowl of rice pudding and reading the latest issue of his favourite music magazine, when Kenny banged through the swinging kitchen doors. Kenny was carrying two big paper bags, presumably to the fellow waiting at the cash—a takeout order—but he stopped dead when he was abreast of Dave's stool. Without turning to look at Dave, standing right behind him, but staring straight ahead at the cash, Kenny said, "That's your second bowl of pudding."

Dave said, "No it isn't."

Kenny said, "It is so. You got up when I was in the kitchen and got yourself a second bowl."

Kenny, who was still looking straight ahead, not at Dave, sounded mildly threatening. Just as Kenny hadn't turned to look at Dave, Dave hadn't turned to look at Kenny.

It was hard to tell if this was a game or something serious. If this were the Wild West, however, you wouldn't take a chance, you'd be looking around for something to duck under in case shooting was about to start. Dave, who had put his spoon down and was staring at his hands, said, "It's *not* my second bowl."

And Kenny said, "Liar."

Everyone in the place stopped talking. Everyone was listening now. There was a beat of silence, some of the customers no doubt thinking *Here come the guns*, when Carl Lowbeer, who was sitting in a booth by the wall, piped up.

Carl said, "It's *not* his second."

Dave spun around on his stool to face Kenny, grinning like a school kid. "See," said Dave.

But Carl wasn't finished. Carl said, "It's his third."

Kenny looked at Carl and then at Dave. "*J'accuse*," he said.

Dave looked over at Carl and muttered, "Traitor."

The tension then proved too much for the guy waiting for his takeout. He grabbed the bags from Kenny's hands and hurried out of the café.

An hour later, the place was mostly empty. Even Carl was long gone. But Dave was still sitting there, still reading his magazine, with a fourth bowl of rice pudding in front of him.

Kenny was there too, with his feet up on his desk, right in the middle of the café. Kenny hung up the phone and said, "Okay. I have been thinking about this … I have decided next Thursday is my fake birthday."

"Ah, come on," said Dave. "We just got through Christmas."

Kenny looked at him sideways. "That's not a protest is it? Is that a protest?"

Dave thought for a second and said, "No, no. I was just saying."

Kenny said, "'Cause if you want to lodge a protest, that's okay with me."

"I was just saying," said Dave. "I wanted you to be sure."

Kenny and Dave have this thing about birthdays. I am not sure how long it has been going. A long time. Once a year, whenever they feel like it, they are allowed to declare that it's their birthday and the other guy has to take fake birthday guy to lunch. And give him a present. According to the rules, they can declare any day of the year their fake birthday, *except*, of course, if it's their *real* birthday, which they are not allowed to mention. They just observe the fake birthday.

And that's how Dave ended up at the mall, looking to find Kenny a fake birthday present. It is something he has been surprisingly good at over the years.

Dave's presents have always been unexpected ... in the best possible way. They have been, when they have been good, something Kenny would never have bought himself, but really wanted nevertheless. And when they have been *great*, well, when they have been great, they have been things Kenny didn't have a clue he wanted, but once he got them wondered how he had lived without them all his life.

Truth is, Kenny looks forward to Dave's fake birthday present every year. Dave knows this, but the great difficulty with great success, of course, is the great difficulty of repeating it. This is why Dave was feeling so much pressure at the mall as he wandered around, looking for inspiration.

He stopped to get a coffee. He was standing at the coffee counter, pouring a creamer into a takeout cup, when he spotted the pet store. And *that* was when Dave remembered the greatest present he had ever bought. Not for Kenny. For his son, Sam.

He had arrived at the mall feeling pleased with himself that year. It was Christmas Eve, and the stores were filled with men, loaded down with parcels, all moving briskly and with purpose.

His first stop was the toy section of a large department store.

"Twelve-year-old girl," he said to the clerk.

The middle-aged woman handed him a brightly packaged craft kit, as if she had been doing this sort of thing all night. Dave paid for the kit and left, not asking for suggestions for Sam. He knew that *he* could figure out the perfect present for a five-year-old boy himself.

Two hours later, he was still stumbling through the mall, past the inappropriately violent toys, past the brightly coloured baby things, overwhelmed by the sea of plastic.

And that was when he stopped for coffee. At the very counter he was stopped at now. He had been standing there, right where he was right now, trying to do what all kids dread their parents doing—trying to come up with a present that wasn't on his son's Christmas list. And it was while he was standing there, only because he was standing there, that he spotted the pet store.

"Perfect," he muttered. So perfect he walked in without taking his coffee with him. So perfect he forgot his coffee on the counter.

He was thinking of something simple as he walked through the door. Thinking goldfish or maybe a turtle. And then he wound around one of the aisles and almost bumped right into Rat Man.

Rat Man, who was pudgy and maybe thirty years old, one of those guys whose belly popped out between the bottom buttons of his shirt, struck Dave as a tad too old for the enthusiasm he seemed to feel about the animals he was displaying, which happened to be … rats.

He was holding three of them. One on his shoulder and two in his hands.

Dave froze, his heartbeat accelerating. Dave happens to be terrified of rats. Phobic almost. He had suffered this for years—ever since the long-ago morning he woke up on Vincent Furnier's couch with a rat perched on his chest. This is God's truth, and goes way, way back; back before Vince changed his name and got famous. Dave woke up on his back with the rat sitting on his chest, nibbling a piece of pizza that Dave had been nibbling himself when he had dozed off.

How was he to know the rat was Vince's pet?

All he knew was that he woke up and he was staring into those beady little eyes. And that now, just the *thought* of rats terrified him. Sometimes he lies in bed at night listening for them, especially if he is in a strange bed, like a hotel or something.

When he got married, Morley had to get used to it. Then she got sick of it. The furnace would bump on and Dave would jerk awake. "Did you hear that?" he'd ask, shaking her.

"Don't worry, sweetie," she'd say, rolling over, "it's only a rat."

Morley was right—the rat thing was out of control. That little seed of fear, planted on Vince's couch so many years ago, had overtaken him. It was long ago, but Dave stood in that pet store as frightened as if it was yesterday.

There were three little boys between Dave and the Rat Man, all of them staring up at him, or more to the point, at his rats: at the rat perched on his shoulder, the rat under his arm and the rat he was holding in his hands.

"Male rats," he was explaining, "are called *bucks*. Females are called *does*. The babies are called *kittens* or *pups*. A group of rats is referred to as a *pack*. Or a *mischief*. I like mischief better. These little guys really love mischief. Come here, Elvis." And with that, he scooped the rat off his shoulder and handed it to one of the kids.

"Don't worry, he won't hurt you. They are very intelligent creatures. Highly intelligent. And highly psychological. In many ways, very similar to us, except cleaner and more playful."

Although Dave didn't want any part of this, he was mesmerized. He wanted to run, but he couldn't stop staring. He stared at the Rat Man. And then at the boys. Each one was holding a rat now. The Rat Man looked at Dave and smiled. He reached out and took a rat away from one of the kids and shoved it toward Dave.

"Interested?" he said.

Dave recoiled in horror.

"Not for me," said Dave. "My son. I was thinking, a turtle."

"You can't get a *turtle*," said the Rat Man, who was now walking toward Dave. "You got to go for something with fur. And a guinea pig is going to bite you soon as look at you."

"What about a hamster?" said Dave, pathetically.

"Hamsters," said the man, "keep you up all night.

"But rats," said the man, pushing the rat toward Dave, "rats are smart, loyal, affectionate and friendly."

None of this sounded like good news to Dave. Not one little bit. He tried to back away.

"Look at these boys," said Rat Man. "Make your boy happy. Believe me."

And maybe, thought Dave, ten minutes later, after he had calmed down a little, *help me master my phobia?*

Before he knew it, Dave was walking out of the pet store with a five-pound bag of cedar shavings and a small cardboard box.

The gift-wrap lady was an older woman, wearing a red reindeer cardigan and snowman earrings.

"It's for my son," said Dave, holding out the box.

The lady smiled as she took it from him. Then the box squeaked, vibrated and leapt in the air.

"Good lord," said the lady, "what *is* this?"

"It's okay," said Dave, trying to reassure her. "It's just a rat."

It took Dave a few minutes and twenty dollars to convince the lady to wrap the rodent. When he got to his car, he checked to make sure the air holes in the gift wrap were still open. Then he placed the wrapped rat on the backseat.

The chewing started a few minutes later.

Dave adjusted the rear-view mirror so he could see into the back. The box was moving around on the back seat like a windup toy. There was a small pink nose popping out of the paper. The rat was chewing its way to freedom.

Dave stepped on the gas. He had to get home quickly. He covered a block and glanced back in the mirror. He could see a nose and whiskers.

A block later there was an entire rat face.

And then there was no rat at all. All that Dave could see was a great empty hole in the box. A hole in the box and a rustling from under his seat. The rat was loose.

Traffic was slowing up ahead. The brake lights on the car in front of him flashed. Dave was so preoccupied he almost missed them. Without thinking, he stepped down on his brake.

Nothing happened.

Well, that's not entirely true. He stepped on the brake and there was a loud squeak. And then Dave felt something rip into his ankle. He looked down. He saw the rat's tail disappearing under his seat.

He pulled over on the side of the road and spent the next ten minutes scrambling around his car—back and forth from front to back, grasping and lunging like he was playing a game of squash. Eventually he got it.

As he felt the wriggling creature in his hand, Dave struggled to make himself hold on and think pleasant, non-phobic thoughts. He thought about how surprisingly soft and warm the rat felt. He thought of the Rat Man, who had no fear. He thought of Sam and how much he would like a rat for Christmas. He did not think about pizza or about Vincent Furnier's couch.

Dave was sitting in the front seat, holding the rat. The rat was quivering. Dave was panting. The box was finished.

If he was going to drive home, he had to put the rat somewhere. Dave looked at the glove compartment. It would be a squeeze. Too tight.

He couldn't drive home with a rat squished into a space designed for a pair of gloves. Whatever he felt about rats, presumably, they had feelings too. What if it was a claustro-phobic rat?

Dave settled on the only other available place: the trunk. There was plenty of room in the trunk. He got out of the car, keys in one hand, rat in the other. He placed the rat beside a box of old records and closed the trunk. He wasn't that far from home. What else could he do?

He pulled away from the curb, but he was anxious. What if the rat was getting bounced around? What if the crate of records slid over and crushed it? Halfway home, he stopped and pulled over. He wanted to check if the rat was okay.

When he opened the trunk, he couldn't see a rat anywhere. And what are you supposed to do about that?

Dave shut the trunk quickly. He felt a wave of dread. It was a visceral response. You lose an umbrella or a wallet, and you feel stupid. You lose a living thing, *any* living thing, and it works on you differently. It merges with all the living things you hold yourself responsible for. He had lost sight of a rat in his trunk—it might as well have been his child in the super-market. He could feel a franticness rising in him.

He was on a residential street, not far from his own neigh-bourhood. He was parked by the curb in the dark spot between two street lights.

Now, there are, in the trunk of any car the size of Dave's, even under the best of conditions, a lot of dark spots, a lot of nooks and a lot of crannies. Not to mention rags and cans and half-full boxes of records. Lots of places where a rat could disappear. Probably the rat was hiding. But maybe it was stuck. Maybe his Christmas gift was in distress, wedged somewhere in a crevice of his trunk, maybe even expiring. Or maybe it had escaped.

He looked down the street anxiously. There was a man at the end of the block walking a dog. But there weren't any rats in sight.

He stood by the trunk and stared at the mess of his life. Why were these things always happening to him? Why wasn't his trunk better organized? *Okay, get a grip*, he thought. *A systematic search. Work from one side to the other.*

And it was while Dave was leaning in on the curb side of his trunk, shifting boxes around, that it occurred to him that the rat could just as easily be on the other side of the trunk, and could just as easily, while Dave was looking here on *this* side, make a break from over *there*, on *that* side.

Without pausing to think about what he was doing, acting rather than thinking, Dave *climbed* into his trunk and reached up and pulled the hood down behind him. No rat was getting out of his trunk unless he *let* him out.

That's what he was thinking when he heard the unmistakable click of the trunk locking shut. His next thought was, *I probably shouldn't have pulled that quite so firmly.*

He reached up in the sudden darkness and pushed against the roof with his hand. Nothing.

"Okay," he said. "Deep breath."

He was going to be okay. He wasn't going to die. He was just locked in the trunk of his car. Lots of people get locked in their trunks. As long as he didn't panic, everything would be just fine.

Two minutes later Dave was thrashing about and yelling and pounding on the roof of the trunk—lurching around in the darkness like a load of laundry on Extra Spin.

It was Christmas Eve. The street was almost empty. An eight-year-old boy and his mother were walking on the opposite side of the road.

"I think," said the boy, pointing at Dave's car, "I think that there is a body in that trunk. I think the body is talking."

The mother reached for her son's hand.

"That's it, young man," she said. "No more TV for you." And they disappeared down the sidewalk.

Inside the dark trunk Dave had stopped his pounding. Inside the trunk Dave was trying to get a grip.

Think. Think. Think. His cellphone. He had his cellphone with him. Why hadn't he thought of that? He squirmed around so he was lying on his back. It was frighteningly dark. He was horribly cramped. But he had his phone.

He worked it out of his pocket and flipped it open. The trunk was bathed in a dim grey light. That was better. He could deal with this.

And then—God help him! There was something staring at him. He was trapped in the trunk, and all he could see was a pair of eyes glaring at him. They were just like those pizza eyes. And they were getting closer.

In his panic he had thrown the phone. Where was his phone? Okay, he had the phone. Who was he going to phone? He certainly wasn't going to phone Morley. The police. He'd call the police.

The call didn't go as smoothly as you might expect. You try explaining to a police dispatcher that you have locked yourself in the trunk of your car because you have climbed in there looking for a rat.

It would have made things a lot easier if Dave knew what

street he was on. He didn't. Well, he wasn't sure. He knew the general vicinity.

The police sent a car. The police officer turned on his siren and drove around the neighbourhood.

"I hear it," said Dave sheepishly. "It sounds like you're a street over."

"Marco," said the cop.

"Polo," said Dave glumly.

Of course there is nothing like a siren to attract a crowd. Or the sight of a police officer prying open a trunk with a crowbar.

"Are you okay, sir?" the office said when he finally popped it open.

Dave, who was lying more or less in the fetal position, nodded earnestly. "I'm just looking for my ra— guinea pig."

He was trying to sound nonchalant. As if this was something he did every day.

The officer put out a hand to help Dave from the trunk. Dave didn't move.   *

Dave said, "Well, I haven't found him yet!"

When he finally struggled out, he was clutching the rat like a child's toy. He smiled ruefully at the gathered crowd. "My guinea pig," he said, holding up the rat.

There was a smattering of applause. But Dave overheard a young woman near the police car say something to her friends.

"Isn't that Stephanie's dad?"

The crowd drifted away. Dave stood by his car as the policeman filed his report. The rat was still quivering. Dave brought it up to his face and blew on its head. The rat nuzzled

Dave's neck. The guy in the pet store was right. It was sort of cute.

He certainly couldn't put it back in the trunk. And the cop wouldn't let Dave drive home with a loose rat in his car.

"Well?" said Dave.

The cop gave Dave and the rat a ride home. But he made them sit in the back, behind the barrier.

As they pulled in to the driveway, Dave could see Sam peering at them through the living-room window. Dave leaned forward in his seat and tapped the barrier lightly.

"Hey," he said to the police officer. "Can you do me one more favour?"

The next morning Sam was so excited about Dave's present that Morley could barely get him to open any other gifts. His father had bought him a rat. And not just any rat. As Sam told everyone, his dad had given him an official, licensed, certified *police* rat. It was delivered in a squad car, by a real police officer. With a badge. It was the *perfect* gift.

And that's what Dave got Kenny for his birthday this year—a rat like Sam's. This time he bought a cage. He gave it to Kenny at lunch. "It's an official police rat," he said.

Kenny said, "What do I want with a rat? I run a restaurant."

Dave smiled. "I'll tell you," said Dave, sitting down at the counter. "Get me a couple of bowls of that rice pudding. It's a long story."

Dear Stuart,

As francophone Canadians, we really appreciate it when you feature French-Canadian history, music and culture on The Vinyl Cafe, *but we do have one question. Not to be too blunt about it, where exactly did you learn to speak French?*

Sincerely,
Michel and Lise

Dear Michel and Lise,

Thanks for your letter. I learned to speak French much the way my young friend Sam did. Except sadly there was no girl.

A TRIP TO QUEBEC

They left on a Monday morning, at 7:30. The annual grade-eight trip to Quebec City. Seven-thirty in the morning and the entire neighbourhood was revved up. All the mothers and fathers. You would have thought they were leaving for war. Jenny Moore, Peter's mother, hovering by the bus with her eyes full of tears and her hands full of Kleenex.

And Jenny wasn't the only one crying—just the most obvious. Jenny was Ping-Ponging from one teacher to another: *Would they remember Peter was allergic to eggs? Was there a bathroom on the bus? She had given him sixty dollars. Yes, she knew it was supposed to be forty, but the extra twenty just in case.*

Peter was already on board. Peter had clambered onto the bus the moment it arrived.

Murphy was second. And when Murphy found out about the extra twenty dollars, he re-appeared out the front door and used the information to pry an additional twenty dollars from *his* father.

All the parents gathered around the kids. All the kids, with their fancy packsacks, ignoring them. There were brothers and sisters, a nanny or two and Mark Portnoy, on the edge of it all, looking lost. The only kid who came by himself. The only kid carrying his stuff in a plastic bag.

Before you knew it, it was time to go. The kids pushed onto the bus and headed for the back, bouncing around the seats and colliding in the aisles. Parent volunteers settled into the seats at the front. And Mr. Reynolds, with his clipboard, stuck his head out the front door, looking up and down the street uncertainly. Sure enough, there they were. Dave and Sam running down the street, backpacks slapping their thighs, Arthur barking as he tried to keep up.

"Sorry," puffed Dave when they got there, "the alarm didn't go off."

Dave had actually volunteered to be one of the parent supervisors. Mr. Reynolds had demurred.

"Oh," lied Mr. Reynolds when Dave had called, "that's very kind. But we already have a full complement."

"Put me down as a backup," said Dave.

Over my dead body, thought Mr. Reynolds.

After months of anticipation, and weeks of planning, they were finally ready. Outside, the parents lined up on either side of the bus and waved at kids they couldn't see through the tinted windows. Inside, the kids couldn't have cared less. When the bus finally pulled away, the two groups of parents found themselves waving at each other. Everyone cracked up, waved even harder and then walked down the street in twos and threes.

Everyone except for Peter's mom. She sprinted to the next corner so she could catch the bus as it turned at the end of the block. Poor Jenny Moore waving all by herself, at no one at all. The only person who saw her was twenty-two-year-old Pierre Massicotte, a second-year social science major at Université Laval. Pierre was sitting in the jump seat in the stairwell to the driver's right. And Pierre was too preoccupied to pay Jenny Moore any mind. Pierre was going over and over the speech he had been preparing all week.

It began like this:

We are going on a fantastic trip. And I want you to leave everything you know behind you. I want you to pretend we are in a boat, not a bus. And I want you to pretend that we have just left France. And just like the French people in the seventeenth century who climbed into their boats, we don't know where we are going or what is going to happen to us.

Pierre was the student guide. And this was his first-ever class trip. He had put a lot of thought and effort into his presentation.

He waited until the bus hit the highway and he stood up and reached for the mic. He took a deep breath.

"We are going to Nouvelle France. And we are going to be there for four days. I want you to be adventurers. I want you to give me your five senses for four days."

Instead of the rapt audience he had imagined, Pierre was greeted with the sounds of candy wrappers ripping, pop cans popping, Game Boys buzzing, iPods leaking, and snoring, from one of the parent volunteers.

Murphy turned to Sam and said, "Last year they went to the IMAX. Do you think we will go to the IMAX?"

The only people listening to Pierre were two girls sitting way up front who said, "*Oui monsieur, oui monsieur,*" right from the start, and who were now poring over Will Ferguson's

Canadian History for Dummies, apparently checking Pierre's facts.

It was not the reception Pierre had imagined. But Pierre didn't give up. Pierre kept going.

"The food we are going to eat is not the same as your parents' food. I want you to *taste* the food. The houses are not your parents' houses. They are made of stone. I want you to *touch* the stone walls. The French and the British built them two to three hundred years ago. I want you to *smell* the horses and buggies, and the smells coming out of the horses."

Someone at the back of the bus made a fart noise and everyone laughed. Then Mark Portnoy put up his hand. "I need to go to the bathroom," he said loudly. And finally, everyone was listening.

"There is a toilet at the back," said Pierre.

"It's gross," said Mark. "Can't we stop at a Tim Hortons?"

The bus broke into applause.

In a few months' time, after a few more trips, Pierre will recognize this kind of interruption as the perfect way to get the kids to listen. "Where," he will ask, in a few more months, "do you think you would go to the bathroom, if you were in Quebec City three hundred years ago?"

That will get their attention. And once he gets it, he will continue.

"You'd go in the same place as the horses—in the street. I want you to smell the horses because that's what it smelled like three hundred years ago. Smell the horses, *taste* the food, *touch* the stones and listen to the language that you will hear all around you."

But this was Pierre's first trip. And he didn't say any of that. Pierre just sighed, and said, "We aren't stopping for another two hours," and he sat down and turned off the PA.

He had lost them. He wasn't getting them back. And he knew it.

By mid-morning they were rolling through the rich and green valley of the Fleuve St-Laurent.

"One of the great rivers of the world," said Pierre. He had been planning on telling all of the students about the river. Instead he was talking to the two girls sitting in the first row.

"Everything else on the continent goes north–south. This river flowing this way," he pointed east along the highway, "made the idea of Canada possible."

"Oh," said one of the girls. She was looking toward the back of the bus. They were watching DVDs back there. Her history text had slipped to the floor.

At Gananoque they left the hustle of Highway 401 for the pastoral beauty of the Thousand Islands Parkway. Pierre pointed at a clump of green islands in the river.

"That's Canada's smallest national park," he said. But the two girls had moved to the back of the bus. He was talking to the bus driver.

They passed Mallorytown, and Butternut Bay, and Cardinal, and they stopped by the Iroquois Lock to eat the picnic lunches their parents had packed them.

"Part of the St. Lawrence Seaway," said Pierre, to no one in particular.

The sky was blue and the clouds were white and the world was perfect—made more so when an impossibly large laker glided through the lock, moving as smoothly as if it were on tracks. The boat was almost close enough to touch.

It was late afternoon before they closed in on Quebec City—North America's only walled city. The breathtaking stone turrets and towers of the Château Frontenac guard the cliffs and cobblestones of old Quebec like an ancient castle. The Gibraltar of America.

Everyone was pressed to a window as the bus rolled onto the Quebec Bridge. Pierre reached for the microphone.

"Longest cantilevered bridge in the world," said Pierre.

He waited until they were high above the river, about halfway across, and added, as if it was just an afterthought, "It has collapsed twice."

That produced the first reaction Pierre got all afternoon.

The hotel that had been booked for the trip was a *pension* inside the walls of the old city. The floors were uneven, the stairways narrow. There was an elevator with a frayed green carpet decorated with gold fleurs-de-lys. The elevator looked as old as the city, and the fleurs-de-lys were like little worn moths. No more than two people with suitcases could ride in the elevator at the same time, and everyone except the two girls from the front of the bus banged their suitcases up the stairs.

The kids were billeted four to a room, two to a bed. They had half an hour to settle in to their rooms and argue about who was going to sleep with whom. Then they were to meet in the lobby.

There were signs on their beds that said *Phone the front*

desk if you need more pillows. The kids felt like royalty. It took about five minutes before the woman at the front desk stopped answering the phone.

When they went downstairs, Pierre circled them up in the lobby. "We have an hour before dinner," he said. "Go explore. No one go alone. And not beyond the Porte Saint-Jean or Rue Ste-Anne."

They couldn't believe it. Sure, most of them had been away from their parents before. A lot of them had even been to camp. But at camp there was always someone watching. At camp they never dropped you in some town and let you wander around unsupervised. It was beyond the realm of their imaginations. They stood in the lobby for a moment in shock. And then off they went. The shy ones stuck to the teachers. But most of them headed off in groups of two and three.

Peter Moore was like a cat let off a leash.

"Come on," he said.

Murphy and Sam followed him out the front door of the hotel and down the street. Murphy led them into the first depanneur they saw.

"I want to get some Red Bull for tonight," said Murphy.

"Look at this," said Peter. Peter was holding the biggest plastic troll doll they had ever seen. It was almost two feet high and had bright-orange hair that stuck out in all directions. Its troll hands were perched on its hips.

Peter said, "Watch this."

The troll's eyes lit up and began to flash.

"There's a button on the back of its head," said Peter. "It's only twenty-one dollars."

At five o'clock they gathered in the hotel lobby and marched off like just another army set on conquering Quebec—up the Côte de la Fabrique, along Rue du Trésor. They stopped at Champlain's statue in the Place d'Armes and then headed along the Rue St-Louis. Pierre pulled up in front of a little stone house with a steep red roof.

"Built in 1677," he said as they marched into a restaurant that was much too good for them. Prix fixe: boeuf bourguignon, salad and dessert.

"This meat looks like dog food," called a voice from the back.

Less than half of them ate their stew. But they all devoured their dessert—sugar pie.

At ten o'clock that night, Mr. Reynolds went from room to room checking that everyone was present and accounted for. He had a roll of masking tape in his pocket. As he left each room, he tossed the masking tape in the air and caught it.

"I'm putting a strip of tape across your door," he said. Then he told them about the all-night security guard. If the guard saw the tape on their door was broken, he would know they had left their room. They didn't want to *know* how much trouble they'd be in if that happened.

"Is the guard *armed*?" asked Peter Moore.

"He has a Kalashnikov," said Mr. Reynolds. "He's Israeli."

Then he said, "Lights off at 10:30. Right?"

"Yes, Mr. Reynolds. Yes, sir. We're pretty tired, sir."

"Good night, boys."

"Good night, Mr. Reynolds."

Ten-thirty? There wasn't a light out by two-thirty. There was much too much do. In Eleanor Michelin's room, four little girls had set up a spa and were attempting to turn the bathroom into a steam room by running the shower at full hot.

Two floors above, in Room 421, Mark Portnoy, the only kid with a bed to himself, was about to show his three goggle-eyed roommates, who were sleeping in the other bed, how to make a blowtorch using a can of hairspray and a cigarette lighter in the shape of a cannon that he had bought on Rue St-Jean.

There was a marathon Xbox tournament getting under way in the room below them.

And on the top floor, in Sam and Murphy's room, there was a two-foot troll being lowered out the window on the curtain sash. At any moment it was going to come even with the window of the girls' room one floor below, its red eyes flashing menacingly.

All of this, of course was happening *behind* the taped doors. So at eleven o'clock, when Pierre reported to Mr. Reynolds that all was quiet, Mr. Reynolds nodded and said, "You can go then."

Mr. Reynolds took a look down the hotel corridor. He wasn't naive enough to believe everyone was asleep. But as long as the kids were in their rooms, Mr. Reynolds was going to try his best not to think too hard about what might be happening in them.

If he had stepped outside for a moment and looked at the hotel from the street, he would have seen that the Pension du Vieux Québec was lit up like a party ship. There was steam billowing from a bathroom. What looked like a flame-thrower was belching occasionally from the fourth floor, and a troll with flashing eyes was dancing around in the night sky.

Mr. Reynolds missed all this, however, and was sound asleep by midnight, which was when Charlotte Groves got bored of her pedicure and picked up the remote control and discovered Canal Deux—the Blue Channel.

It was Eleanor Michelin who worked out how you could phone from room to room without going through the switchboard, and word spread like wildfire. Pretty soon every television in every room was switched to Canal Deux, and the educational component of the trip to Quebec began in earnest.

"*That's not real*, is it?" said Peter Moore, moving closer to the television.

The next morning, Peter snuck back to the depanneur during breakfast and spent every last cent of his lunch money on troll dolls. When Sam and Murphy came back upstairs to clean up, Peter had his trolls, all sizes and shapes, lined up on the windowsill like soldiers. There were seventeen of them.

"Peter," said Murphy. "I can't believe you have done this. What are you going to do for food?"

Peter didn't care. It was hours until lunch. Peter was lost on Planet Troll. "Look at this one," said Peter. "Isn't it cool?"

"Come on," said Sam. They were supposed to be in the lobby.

They followed Pierre through Place d'Armes, and past the château, and onto the wide wooden boardwalk suspended high above the river. To the east, in the lee of the Île d'Orléans, you could see that the great colonies of snow geese had begun to gather. Pierre was about to stop and point them out—from this distance they looked like slashes of snow on the shore—but then decided to let it pass, thinking, as he kept walking, that winter was closer than he had realized.

It was in the Jardin des Gouverneurs that he had his brainstorm.

"Come on," he said. He was taking them to the Plains of Abraham.

"*Venez. Venez. Dépêchez-vous,*" said Pierre.

He divided them into two armies and assigned them roles. Murphy was Governor General Vaudreuil. Peter, the Intendant Bigot. Sam was General Wolfe.

"What are we doing?" said Murphy.

"We are going to recreate the battle," said Pierre. "You," he said, pointing at Mark Portnoy. "You can be the Marquis de Montcalm."

"I don't want to be Montcalm," said Mark. "He lost. We ..."

"*We* what?" said Pierre. "Who do you mean ... *we?*"

Mark Portnoy shrugged. "Canada," he said.

"Canada?" said Pierre. "There was no Canada then."

They were standing on the green Plains of Abraham, just outside the walls of the citadel. For the first time Pierre had everyone's attention.

"This wasn't," said Pierre sweeping his arm around him, "this wasn't a battle between English Canada and French Canada. There was no English Canada. There were *British* ships, and *British* troops. Were *they* the Canadian army? They weren't the Canadian army. There was no Canadian army.

"This was a European war that was fought here. Canada came later. Canada hadn't been invented. Not yet."

They re-fought the battle three times. Everyone jumping and shooting and whooping around. Twice the British won. And once, to make it fair, the French carried the day, Mark Portnoy stomping back and forth, with his fist in the air.

After the battle Murphy, all grass stained and sweaty, ran up to Pierre.

"That was pretty cool," said Murphy. "But are we going to go to the IMAX ... like last year?"

"Tomorrow," said Pierre, defeated. "We *are* going to the IMAX tomorrow."

Murphy pumped his fist in the air.

"Yes," said Murphy.

News spread like wildfire. This was going to be great. The highlight of the trip. NASCAR 3-D! In French.

They left for the theatre the next morning at ten. As everyone staggered onto the bus, Sam wheeled around and looked at Murphy. "I forgot my wallet," he said patting his back pocket. "I'll be right back."

He peeled out of the bus and into the hotel.

Murphy was never able to explain what happened next. But what happened was clear.

Mr. Reynolds did attendance. And when he called Sam's name and Sam wasn't there to answer, Murphy answered for him. If he had thought about it for a moment, he wouldn't have done it. It was a gut reaction. He didn't want Sam to get in trouble. And then before he could think of anything, he heard Mr. Reynolds say, "All present. Let's roll." And Murphy panicked. He should have run to the front and stopped the bus. But he hesitated.

Meanwhile Sam, who had bounded through the hotel lobby as fast as he could, had hit the sidewalk. But it was four floors up and four floors down. And when he got there, he stopped dead in his tracks. He couldn't believe his eyes. The bus had left without him.

Murphy had tried to keep him out of trouble and there he was all alone, on Rue St-Jean. In trouble.

Sam stood in front of the hotel for about five seconds. He felt a surge of panic, and then he did the only thing he could think of doing. He started running in the direction the bus had been pointing.

There was a red light, and he spotted it a block away, but the light changed and the bus was accelerating, and even though he did too, even though, fuelled by fear and his desire not to miss the movie, Sam ran harder than he had ever run in his life, running even when he couldn't see the bus anymore, he lost it, and eventually pulled up, standing in the middle of a block, bent over, his hands on his thighs. A spent little NASCAR clean out of fuel.

When Sam straightened up he saw a policeman on the other side of the street and he almost asked him the way to the theatre, but it occurred to him the cop wouldn't just give him directions. He would make calls that would certainly get him in trouble.

So he didn't ask the cop. Instead, he asked the boy carrying the skateboard. It was only after he'd asked that he realized the boy was a girl. And by then, she was as confused as he was. Because as far as this girl understood, this odd-looking boy she had never seen before had just asked her on a date to the IMAX.

Sam had used his best French, but it had come out fast and garbled.

"*Quoi?*" said the girl he thought was a boy.

Sam wanted to start running again, but it was too late to start running again, and anyway where was he going to run? So he tried again.

The girl was leaning forward, looking at him really hard, and then she said, "Ahh." She started talking in French, and she was going so fast that he didn't understand a word. Not one word.

And she must have seen that because she stopped talking and said, "*C'est trop difficile*. It is too far from here. You can't do it. It is much too *difficile*."

"I have to," said Sam. "Everyone is there. I can't miss it. Everyone is there." His voice cracked. "It's the best thing of the trip." He was still out of breath. He was thinking, I am not going to cry. I can't cry.

The girl shrugged.

"*C'est difficile*," she said again. "*Mais*, I could show you there."

And he wasn't sure, but maybe she reached out and wiped a tear off his cheek, or maybe he just wanted her to.

She was wearing black boots, brown army pants way too big for her and a baggy jacket. They were walking beside each other now and she was saying, "Where are you to?" Sam said, "The movie theatre." The girl looked at him funny, and he understood that she meant *from*, where was he *from*. And he said, "Toronto. I am from Toronto."

"Oh," she said. "I am so sorry."

And then she was climbing up on the wall. On the wall that went around the city. Sam was standing there below her. He didn't know what to say next. So he said, "I am on school trip." And she, "*Je sais. Je sais.*" Sam and the girl stared at each other without moving. Then she waved her arms in exasperation and said, "*Viens, viens.* It's okay."

And before Sam knew it, they were walking along the old stone wall of the city, thirty feet in the air, the street on their left, the river on their right, as if they were walking along railway tracks. Sam said, "We drove past this yesterday."

And then he told her about the Plains of Abraham, and the museum, and Peter's trolls. He was talking to her back because she was ahead of him by a couple of steps; he was telling her how he had left his wallet in his room.

Eventually, the girl slowed down and they were walking beside each other. She said, "Did you see the cannonball in the tree?"

Sam said, "Which one?"

The girl stopped walking and said, "It's super cool."

She jumped off the wall; and the way she jumped holding her skateboard over her head was almost as cool as the way she said "super cool." Sam stood there staring at her.

"*Viens*," she said again.

Sam jumped down off the wall and the two of them ran down the narrow cobbled streets hand in hand.

Well, that's how Sam imagined they ran. In truth, the girl ran in front of him, and Sam had to push himself to keep up. He had forgotten all about the IMAX.

"*Tiens*," she said pointing. Sure enough there was a cannonball, at the edge of a narrow lane, the roots of a tree gnarled around it.

He smiled at her and said, "Super cool." Then he said, "I was General Wolfe in the battle."

Suddenly he remembered she was French and felt awkward and added, "It was just a play. Montcalm won once."

And she said, "I saw Montcalm's skull."

The way she said it he knew it was true. Though the truth is he would have believed *anything* she told him. But the skull of Montcalm! He was so mesmerized he started speaking fluent French.

"*Où?*" he said.

And the most magical thing was that she understood him this time. She said, "*Au musée des Soeurs Ursulines.*"

And off they went again, over another cobblestone hill to another museum to see the skull of Louis-Joseph le Marquis de Montcalm.

When they got there, Sam said, "*Moi, je n'ai jamais vu un crâne.*"

Well, actually, he said, "I have never seen a skull." But talking to *her* it *felt* like he'd said it in French.

The woman in the ticket booth said, "We don't have it anymore. They buried it with his troops in the *basse ville* five years ago."

"Too bad," said the girl. "It was a cute skull."

Sam said, "*Ça fait rien.*"

"*Veux-tu un chocolat chaud?*" she said.

"*Oui,*" he said noticing, with relief, that he had his French back.

They went into a little café on Rue Couillard.

She had a coffee that came in a little cup. His hot chocolate was served in a bowl. He didn't know how you were supposed to drink hot chocolate when it came in a bowl. To be safe he went to the counter and got a spoon. He ate it like soup.

She wanted to ask, *Is that the way the English do it?* But she didn't want him to think she was ignorant. The rest of his manners seemed perfect. *Maybe we do it wrong*, she thought.

Instead of asking him about chocolate, she said, "*Aimes-tu Daniel Belanger?*"

He shrugged.

"*Avril Lavigne?*"

They had to take a bus to the theatre. They sat at the back. He could feel her leg against his. He couldn't think of anything to say to her, so they barely said anything. It took about half an hour.

When they got to the IMAX theatre, the big tour bus was parked outside. Sam said, "That's my bus."

There were kids getting on it.

The girl said, "I think you missed your movie."

Sam said, "I can't miss my bus."

All he wanted to do in all the world was kiss her. He had never done that before. They stared at each other. That's what she wanted too. She wanted him to lean forward and kiss *her* goodbye.

Instead they shook hands.

Murphy said the movie was amazing.

Murphy said, "I can't believe you missed it. It was the best thing I have ever seen."

Sam was looking out the bus window. The girl was standing there with her skateboard under her arm, her head to the side.

Sam said, "I'll see it some other time."

He lifted his hand and waved, tentatively. The girl was looking right at him, squinting at him, but she didn't wave back. She couldn't see him through the tinted windows.

So he brought his hand up to his lips and blew her a kiss.

If he had been older, he would have asked her name and her email or something. And if she had been older, he wouldn't have had to ask.

He didn't know anything about her, really. Except she had seen Montcalm's skull. And he hadn't.

The last moment Sam saw her, Murphy was sitting beside him telling him something about the movie, but he wasn't listening. He had his face pressed to the window. He said something under his breath and Murphy said, "I can't hear you."

And Sam said, "Nothing. It's okay."

And then he turned back to the window and said it again. "*Au revoir*," he said. "*Salut*."

And then just before the bus turned the corner, she blew him a kiss. He leaned back in his chair and sighed.

It was his first kiss.

It was a French kiss.

Dear Stu,

Can I call you Stu? I feel as if I know you already.

I recently went to the local theatre where your Vinyl Cafe *show was on tour. I didn't actually go in, mind you. I find your voice kind of irritating. But I noticed that you drew quite a crowd, and that got me thinking.*

You wouldn't have any extra money that you could lend me, would you?

Awaiting your generosity,
Ted

Dear Ted,

There is no one here by that name. You might find the following story helpful, however.

NEWSBOY DAVE

The door to days gone by is a strange little door, and it can pop open at the oddest moments. When it does that—pops open—unbidden, and spills the light of memory at your feet, you know that almost always you are going to walk through the door, even though you are well aware that once you do, there is no telling the strange places you might go.

Dave was alone in his record store the last time memory came calling. It was a rainy afternoon, and you could tell it was going to be slow. An interlude. But Dave had anything but yesterdays on his mind. He was using the unexpected solitude to flip through a couple of boxes of albums he had been meaning to go through for weeks. Dave was firmly rooted in the here and now.

He was sorting the records into piles on the counter in front of him: a pile for the albums he would keep, a pile for the ones that would sell and a pile for the ones which would go into the bin at the back of the store—*Vinyl's Last Stop*—two dollars an album. He had been at it for over an hour.

He had stopped to make a pot of tea, and he had just begun again, just picked up the very next album, and there it was— the little door of memory, and it was already way too late to do anything about it. The door was wide open, and Dave was already through it.

"Oh my," he said, "Appaloosa."

He hadn't seen the album for fifteen years. Maybe twenty. He glanced, instinctively, at the old green file cabinet under the till. He had a folder in there, somewhere, with letters from people who wanted this record. He already had it out of the jacket, spinning it around to see what kind of shape it was in. Far better than it should have been. He put it on his turntable, of course. And that was the end of that afternoon.

Appaloosa only ever made the one album—jazzy and violiny, a path back to those days when Donovan, and Tim Hardin, and Gordon Lightfoot, and all those coffee house guys were reaching back and jazzing up their folk songs with baroque sounds. Dave's old buddy Al Kooper had produced it. How many years since he had seen Al?

Al, who had famously insinuated himself into the studio during the recording of Bob Dylan's "Like a Rolling Stone."

Dave refilled his mug and leaned back, the Appaloosa jacket propped in his lap. He reached over and turned the volume up. He was listening to Appaloosa, but he was thinking of Al.

Al, who was maybe twenty-one at the time, had brought his guitar to the studio hoping he might be asked to play with Dylan. He put the guitar away as soon as he heard the prodigious Mike Bloomfield warming up. He was watching from the control room when the guy playing the B3 moved over to the piano, and he just couldn't resist. He snuck onto the studio floor when the producer was on the phone. Al didn't really know *how* to play the organ. Al was a guitar player. But when it was all over and they were mixing the cut, Dylan kept saying, "Turn up the organ."

Al once told Dave he wouldn't have been able to turn *on* the organ if someone hadn't already done it.

"If you listen carefully," he said, "you can hear me coming in late on a lot of the changes."

That is because Al was being careful he had the chords right before he played them.

Dave looked up. Side one of the Appaloosa record had been over for a couple of minutes, the needle as lost in the groove of memory as he was.

He flipped the jacket onto the counter, walked to the back of his store and grabbed Dylan's *Highway 61 Revisited*. And he listened to *that* all the way through. And then to Blood Sweat and Tears' first album, which was Al's work too. Heck, Blood Sweat and Tears was Al's band, although he left them before they broke. When *that* album was over, he tried to phone Al at Berkeley. He was teaching there last Dave had heard. But all Dave got was an answering machine. By then it was time to close anyway, so he hung up without leaving a message, switched everything off and went home.

That night, after supper, Dave sat down at the computer and spent several hours drifting around, like a little lost boat on the foggy lake of memory. Appaloosa had led him to Al. Al was leading him all over the place.

Morley was asleep by the time Dave crawled into bed. He was tempted to wake her, but he didn't. He could wait until morning.

When Morley opened her eyes, there he was. He didn't say, Good morning.

Instead of *Good morning*, he said, "Guess what I found on the net last night?"

Morley sat up and squinted at him. "My gloves?" she said.

"A 1973 Gottlieb Deluxe Hot Shot," said Dave. "The one with the green background."

"A what?" said Morley.

It was only the greatest pinball game ever made—way better than the later version with the *blue* background.

"It's for sale," said Dave.

Only about twenty Hot Shots were distributed in North America. It was a game of pinball pool, set in a twenties-style pool hall. There was a quirk, however, in one of the relays—so it gave you a free game if you hit the eight ball directly after the three ball. Well, it didn't take long for everyone to figure *that* out, and for store owners to notice that they weren't making any money on the games. So the manufacturer recalled the machines and never reissued them. A few, however, had slipped through the cracks.

Morley rolled out of bed and headed for the bathroom. Dave rolled out of bed and followed her.

"Beauty of the Hot Shot," said Dave, following Morley into the bathroom, "is you can service it yourself. You just open it up, adjust a rubber band or two and oil the relays and wheels."

Morley was putting toothpaste on her toothbrush. She stopped and turned and stared at Dave in disbelief. Dave mistook it for a look of wonder.

That's what he was feeling. Wonder-full. "If any lights burn out, you can replace them with bulbs you can pick up at a hardware store. Cheap."

Morley said, "Imagine that."

"I know," said Dave, holding out his hand for the toothpaste.

He was still talking at supper—explaining how the Hot Shot was the game that he and Al Kooper had played the autumn they did that college tour, the one along the northeastern seaboard. They lugged the game around in the sound truck and set it up backstage every night.

They played for hours—after every show—under the dark stands of countless sports arenas. People would hang around and watch, using the game's glass top as a counter for their beers. Their whoops, and the machine's chunks, bells and flashing lights echoing through the empty hallways.

The Hot Shot was bright and it was loud.

"Oh, joy," said Morley.

Dinner was over. They were washing the dishes and he was *still* going on. Morley had had enough. She put her towel down and headed into the living room.

And Dave, who hadn't done the pots yet, followed her, wiping his hands on his pants. He was trying to remember the name of the sound guy who used to play by himself after Al and Dave had finished. He was a true artist, fabulous to watch. He would play quietly without saying a word, hardly moving. "It's a Zen thing," he said. "You have to *not* try. You have to *allow* the balls to go where they want to go."

He finally said it.

"I want to buy that pinball game," he said.

"No problem," said Morley. "We can pay for it out of the grocery money."

That shut him up. That put a damper on the fire of his enthusiasm. But it didn't put the fire out.

Dave tended the embers. He kept thinking of the game when he should have been thinking of other things—remembering for instance the time he convinced Al that he had paid Marie-Rose, the Haitian tour cook, twenty-five dollars to put a curse on him.

Dave had ridden in the back of the sound truck that day all the way from Portland, Maine, to Burlington, Vermont. He had spent the trip doctoring the machine. He had opened it up and removed the five regulation stainless steel balls and replaced them with slightly smaller ones. Balls that moved faster, were harder to control, evaded the flippers and went down the gutter more easily.

That night, he let Al go first. Everyone knew what was going on except Al. And there was Al pounding on the flippers in exasperation, Dave standing beside him as calm as could be.

"Try another game, Al. There's no hurry."

The next day Marie-Rose sat at the big table by the cook trailer, working on a plate of chicken and rice. She tilted her head toward Al and said, "He paid me fifty bucks. You want that I should remove the curse?"

They had so much fun. How often could you go back to your boyhood? He couldn't let the machine slip through his fingers.

The idea to *pay* for the pinball game by getting a second job came to him while he was walking to work.

He could have come up with the money. It wasn't about the money. It was the principle. Morley was right—the pinball thing was extracurricular. So, he'd get an extracurricular job to pay for it. A part-time job.

The idea of working for the game pleased Dave enormously. The job would have to be something completely different from what he did day to day. That way there could be no question about where the money came from. Something simple, some-thing contained. He considered all sorts of ideas. He considered house painting. He considered driving a cab. He considered delivering pizzas. All *good* ideas, but not perfect ideas. If he was going to do this, it had to be perfect.

He thought of the perfect idea at lunch.

He wanted to buy something from his boyhood? He should get a boyish job. What could be more boyish than a paper route? Perfect on every level. It would get him up in the morning. He would get some much-needed exercise. He would make the money he needed. And he would fulfill a boyhood ambition.

Dave had never had a part-time job. When he was a kid, he had always wanted to be a paper boy. But in Big Narrows, the town where Dave grew up, the Boxer brothers had a lock on the town's one paper route. As each brother outgrew the route, he passed it on, like a peerage, to the next brother in line. The summer he was twelve, Dave was woken every morning by the creak of Peter Boxer's bicycle. Dave would wake up and lie in bed waiting for the creaking to pause, waiting for the whir and slap of the paper, as Peter tossed it over their fence and onto their porch. As if *Peter* was in charge of waking him, in charge of waking the whole town.

Dave was stomping along the street, grinning foolishly as the kaleidoscope of summers past twisted through his head.

He would get a paper route.

Rising early to deliver papers would be like closing a circle. It would be a return to a simpler time. It would be more than a return to a simpler time. In the midst of his busy life, it would be like one of those things monks do, like bookbinding, or bread making. Delivering papers would be a meditation. His practice. Like the arrows let loose by the Zen archers in that book Al Kooper had given him. It wouldn't be his role to *deliver* the papers—the *natural* state of the papers was *on* the front porches—his contribution would be to release the papers so they could deliver themselves. The paper route would bring patience into his life. Not to mention a pinball game.

He hadn't applied for a job for years. He would need a resumé. It took him all day to get it down to two pages. A man from the paper called three days later.

"We got your resumé," said the man. "Sorry, we only hire adults these days."

"I *am* an adult," said Dave.

"Oh," said man. Dave could hear him shuffling paper.

"I *own* the store," said Dave.

"Oh," said the man again.

They had a route in his neighbourhood. Dave could start Monday morning. It was only after he had hung up that he realized the best thing of all about the job—by doing this he was going to be setting an example for his children. He would be *living* a principle that he had always tried to *teach* them: the important principle of delayed pleasure. If you wanted something, you had to earn it before you could enjoy it.

He received his route by fax on Friday afternoon. He knew many of the people on it. He sat down to talk to Sam on Sunday night. When he had finished explaining everything, he sat back and smiled. Sam didn't say a word. Sam was staring at him.

Dave said, "I know that's a lot to take in. But what do you think of all that?"

Sam said, "You're going to deliver papers so you can buy a pinball machine, right?"

Dave smiled. "Yes, that's right."

Sam said, "Like walking around the neighbourhood *delivering* them door to door?"

Dave said, "Yes."

Sam said, "Our neighbourhood?"

Dave said, "Yes."

Sam said, "That is so ... embarrassing."

The next morning, his first on the job, Dave woke up five minutes before his alarm. It was still dark out. He reached out and turned off the alarm before it rang, so it wouldn't wake Morley.

He had laid out his clothes the night before: his green sweatshirt, a beige spring jacket and a pair of sandals. He figured the sandals would force him to move slowly. He whispered into the kitchen and boiled water for tea. Slowly.

He filled a stainless steel Thermos with the tea and added milk. Slowly. He was moving like a monk.

He was supposed to pick up his papers at Lawlor's Drug Store. When he got there, he would sit quietly and drink his tea before he set off.

When he arrived at Lawlor's, he was surprised to find he was not alone. A man was there already, throwing stacks of newspapers into the back of a little red car. This man was moving quickly, urgently actually, loading hundreds of papers into his car. The driver's door was open and the tape machine was playing some kind of Asian music. The man was small and dark haired. He looked Vietnamese, maybe. He heaved the last bundle onto the passenger seat, leaned over and snipped the bundle open with a pair of wire clippers. Then he nodded curtly at Dave, jumped into his car and peeled off.

There were two small packs of papers left. Dave figured they must be his piles. They were bound together with wire. No one had said anything about wire. Dave tried to work the pile open with his hands. No one could have broken open the pile with their hands.

Dave ran home. Or he tried to run home. It is hard running when you are wearing monk's sandals. He sort of skipped home, bounding down his street like a panicked antelope jumping across the African veldt.

Of course, *Mr. Early Riser*, Bert Turlington, was already up and standing in his driveway.

"You okay?" said Bert as Dave lurched by.

Dave pitched to a stop.

"Wire cutters," he gasped. "I need wire cutters." His heart

was pounding. Little flecks of spit sprayed Bert. "For my paper route."

It was 8:30 before he got home from his rounds. At noon he received a call from the circulation department.

"We received two late complaints," said the lady. "One from number fifty-four and one from fifty."

Dave was indignant. Number fifty-four was his neighbourhood nemesis, Bert's wife, Mary Turlington. Number fifty was *his* house. Morley had called in a complaint.

Dave set the alarm half an hour earlier on Tuesday. He jumped into his clothes and hustled out to the garage. He didn't stop to make tea. He had uncovered Sam's old wagon the night before. He rounded the corner and was in sight of Lawlor's, pulling the wagon behind him, when he realized he had forgotten the wire cutters. The Asian paper carrier was nowhere in sight.

It was raining on Wednesday morning.

Dave did his best to cover the papers in his wagon with a green garbage bag. But the bag kept flapping loose and the edges of the papers kept getting wet.

Then, when he turned the corner, there was a worm stretched across the sidewalk like a rubber band. Dave stopped dead. If he kept going, he would run over the worm with his wagon. He stared at the worm for a long moment. Then he bent over and picked it up. Standing there not sure what to do, Dave dropped the worm into the wagon with the papers. He would put it in his garden when he got home.

In that simple act, Dave made himself responsible for every

drowning worm stretched out on the sidewalk in front of him. He looked down the street. There seemed to be hundreds. How could he spare one worm and not the others? He spent the rest of the route, bobbing up and down the streets like a woodpecker.

The lady from circulation called at noon. Mary Turlington had called again. She had found worms in her paper.

Dave was determined to get better at this. That was the purpose of a practice. He bought a box of thick elastic bands and on Wednesday afternoon went into the backyard with a couple of old papers. He rolled the papers into cylinders and used the elastics to secure them. He set a cardboard box near the back fence. He practised throwing the papers at the box from the far end of the yard, smiling every time he made a direct hit. He was working in the zone until Sam came outside and said, "Couldn't you wait until the sun goes down?"

Thursday morning was as perfect as a morning could be. The sky was warm and blue and dotted with quiet clouds. It hadn't rained. There were no worms to worry about. Dave was pulling his wagon along the sidewalk happily, stopping every time he had a paper to toss. But his release was off. His tosses were falling short. Dave had imagined his papers smacking onto porches and sliding right up to front doors. They were, instead, bouncing up walks, resting on porch stairs. He put more muscle into his next toss. It was still short. So at the next house he eyeballed the door. Standing on the sidewalk, he tried to visualize the throw. He cocked his arm like a discus thrower and let the paper fly, his arm following through. His eyes locked on the paper as it soared through the air and over the front lawn. And then, as it arced over the stairs, he blinked and wondered why the front door was opening. He watched in disbelief as the door opened wide, and his paper smacked Mary Turlington in the face.

The next morning, Carl Lowbear leaned out his bedroom window and called to him. "Hey, Dave," said Carl, "do you want to come over and play after school?"

Slowly, however, things got better. Dave bought himself a retro canvas delivery bag—the kind paper boys carried over their shoulders when he was a kid. It had the word *NEWS* in faded letters on the side. He loved the bag.

One day, when he got to Lawlor's, his stack of papers was twice as big as it had ever been before.

"Flyer day," said the Asian guy.

Dave nodded, sat on the curb and got to work. Right away he realized he had a problem. The first elastic he tried to slip around the fat paper snapped; the next one snapped and zinged him in the eye. It took him twice as long as usual to fill his bag, the elastics zinging around like horseflies. And when the bag was full, there was still a pile of papers left over that wouldn't fit in.

He set off with the bag over one shoulder and the extra papers stuffed under his other arm, hobbling along, struggling to keep everything square. Sections kept slipping out. He had to backtrack to pick up rogue bits and pieces.

When he got to the first house on his route, he pulled a paper out of his bag and launched it at the front porch. The heavy paper stuffed with flyers made it halfway across the lawn before it exploded in mid-air like a spaceship in some intergalactic battle.

Bits of paper flew everywhere—littering the yard with advertisements for home renovations and pizza delivery. It took Dave almost five minutes to bump around and pick it all up. As he lurched down the street, he was aware of Howard Kelman standing in his upstairs bedroom window shaking his head.

The next morning, Howard let his vicious little Pomeranian out the front door just as Dave reached their walk. The dog tore toward Dave like a heat-seeking missile. It stopped inches away from him, jumping backward and forward, snapping at Dave's ankles. As Dave sprinted down the street, his newspaper bag thumping into his hip, Howard called out, "Sorry." But it didn't sound as if he was sorry. It sounded as if he was laughing.

The last Friday of the month was collection day, which should have been easy enough. Most of the people on Dave's route paid for their papers by credit card. There were only two people who paid by cash—only two people he had to collect from. The first was Eleanor Marrotte, an eighty-seven-year-old widow who refused to use credit cards.

Eleanor paid him entirely in change. She counted it out coin by coin, and then as Dave turned to leave, she nudged him and pressed a quarter into his hand.

"This is for you," she said.

The other person who didn't use a credit card was, of course, Mary Turlington.

As Dave stood on the Turlingtons' porch about to ring their bell, he was hating his life. He was hating his life. He was hating his life.

Things weren't working out the way he had imagined. His mornings were rushed—not relaxing at all. His feet were sore and his shoulder ached from the newspaper bag. And worse, he was doing a lousy job. Each day, the silent, swift-moving Asian guy was a reminder of that.

One morning the papers weren't there. Dave got to Lawlor's and the Asian guy was sitting on the sidewalk in Lawlor's doorway.

The guy held up his cellphone and said, "Printing problem. No paper for an hour."

Dave wasn't sure what to do.

The Asian guy said, "You want go coffee?"

Dave hadn't expected that.

The man's name was Thanh Trang. He was from Vietnam.

"Thanh?" said Dave. "Or Trang?"

"Thanh," said the man, waving his hand over his head. "Means *colour of sky.*"

Dave followed his arm across the sky. It was a beautiful morning. White clouds congregating over the city like a pack of puffy elephants. They walked to Kenny Wong's café. All they saw along the way was a bread truck and a lone taxi. They crossed the street wherever they wanted without looking. The only other pedestrian they saw was Emil, carrying a cardboard box with a plant in it down the other side of the street.

Thanh and Dave ordered eggs, toast, orange juice and

coffee. Dave didn't ask how Thanh had made it to Canada. He knew the stories of the Vietnamese boat people: the fearsome South China Sea; the leaky, terrifying, crowded boats; the typhoons; the Thai pirates; the corrupt refugee camps.

"What did you used to do?" asked Dave. "In Vietnam?"

Thanh told Dave he was a doctor in Vietnam.

"Here," he said, "I am not able to practise."

He said this without rancour or frustration.

Thanh said he had two jobs. He worked days in a restaurant and nights as a cleaner.

"Three jobs, then," said Dave.

"Two," said Thanh, counting them off on his fingers. "One, restaurant. Two, cleaner."

"And three," said Dave. "Papers. The papers make three."

"Papers not a real job," said Thanh. He was smiling. "I do papers on way to restaurant."

Then he said, "How many job you have?"

We are, all of us, ultimately, insignificant against the creaking and turning of this old world. But mostly, as the world turns, we are too busy to face the truth of the thing.

Dave took a deep breath. He felt foolish. He felt juvenile. He felt diminished sitting across from this quiet man.

"Hardly one job," he said. "I own a little record store."

"You do papers on way to store?" said Thanh.

"Just for a while," said Dave. "Just for a couple of months. Until I can buy something."

"Me too," said Thanh. "I want to buy new washing machine and dryer for my wife. Then maybe new fridge."

Dave took a deep breath.

"I want to buy a pinball game," he said.

"What?" said Thanh.

"A pinball game," said Dave.

Thanh obviously didn't know what he was talking about. Dave was tempted to let that go. But if this guy deserved anything, he deserved the truth.

How to explain this? He held his arms out in front of him as if he were working the flippers. "A machine," he said. "A game. There is a ball and ..."

"I know pinball," said Thanh, exasperated.

Oh. Dave had misinterpreted the look on Thanh's face. Thanh wasn't confused. He was ... disappointed.

Dave said, "It's just a game."

Thanh said, "I know. I know. What game?"

"Oh," said Dave. "It's called the Hot Shot. It is a game, where you ... it's a game like pool ..."

"Blue or green background?" said Thanh.

And in that moment, right then, right there, they became friends—sitting in the booth of Kenny Wong's café on that beautiful and soft morning before anybody else was up. They talked about music.

"Blood Sweat and Tears," said Thanh. "My favourite group."

Al Kooper's band. Al put Blood Sweat and Tears together.

The game arrived three months later, on a truck from Indianapolis. It came on a Thursday, but Dave waited for Sunday to set it up—when the record store wasn't open and Thanh wasn't working. Delayed pleasure. Is there any better?

He invited Thanh and his family to the store. Morley and

Sam joined them. They ordered dinner, and then everyone played Hot Shot.

Dave and Thanh started off. They were both horrible. Tilting the machine all over the place, completely blowing games.

"I thought you said you were good," said Thanh.

"Ah," said Dave, "Once. It will take a while to get the feel back."

He had always thought the thrill of pinball was being in "the zone," playing well, getting the game lit up like a Christmas tree. But pinball never made him as happy as that Sunday evening, sitting in his store with Thanh Trang and his wife, as they passed around boxes of Kenny Wong's crispy salt cod, while his son, Sam, leaning against the machine, watched Thanh's twelve-year-old daughter, Sarah, pull the plunger back and put a ball into play. Sam was staring at Sarah's face, not at the game, and not at the flashing lights or the clunking bells. He was completely unconscious of all that, and of all the laughter filling Dave's little store.

Dear Stuart,

My wife and I are trying to figure out what we should do with our twelve-year-old son this summer. He is not interested in summer camp, and he certainly won't have a babysitter. My wife and I both work full-time. I think that my son is old enough to stay on his own at the house while we are at work. We have neighbours who can check in with him, and he has a few friends to keep him company. But my wife is worried that he might get into some kind of shenanigans. She listens to your show every week and seems to trust you. Maybe you could share a word or two that would reassure her.

Yours,
Jeff Anderson

Dear Jeff,

Maybe not.

THE WATERSLIDE

It was the dog days of summer and half the city was away. Even the mailman was on vacation. The neighbourhood was so quiet you could hear the spiders at work. There was absolutely *nothing* to do.

Murphy and Sam were lying on their backs, shoulder to shoulder, underneath Jim Scoffield's mulberry tree. There was an ant crawling across Sam's forehead. Both boys had their mouths stretched wide open.

Sam said, "This is crazy. It's been, like, an hour. "

Murphy said, "It's been ten minutes. Do you give up?"

Sam said, "Do you?"

They had a bet. The first one to catch a mulberry in his mouth won.

A hot wind rustled the branches of the tree above them. The boys, sun dappled, watched the leaves turn from green to grey to green again. The clouds were doing summer things, but the berries weren't. Nothing was coming down.

It was the middle of the week in the middle of the summer. The neighbourhood had been reduced to sun, soft wind and one lovelorn cicada vibrating at the top of the mulberry tree.

Murphy said, "It sounds like in *To Kill a Mockingbird*."

Sam said, "Once again I have no idea what you are talking about."

Murphy said, "The cicadas. Do you give up?"

Sam sat up abruptly. Sam said, "Okay. Whatever."

Murphy said, "I win."

Sam and Murphy were in the park. In the little kids' section. They were by the wading pool, draped listlessly over two of the swings. They were barely moving and all alone, except for a bored teenage girl who was pushing a toddler on the swing nearest the gate. The toddler, who was holding an orange Popsicle, was wearing diapers and nothing else.

A water truck swished down the street. They all looked up hopefully as it passed, as if it were going to stop and offer some relief from the heat. But it didn't even slow down. It was there and it was gone, and when it was gone the electric rattle of the neighbourhood cicadas was all that was left. You couldn't tell where they were. It sounded as if they were everywhere.

Sam said, "Cicadas, right?"

Murphy said, "Good. They live underground for seventeen years. Then, on the very same day, they all crawl out of the ground together, and climb to the top of the trees."

Sam said, "They live underground."

Murphy said, "Seventeen years."

Sam said, "What do they live on?"

Murphy said, "Root juice."

Sam said, "And then they all crawl out together. At the same time. After seventeen years."

Murphy said, "They only live for thirty days after that. They lay eggs, die and it all starts again."

Sam said, "If I was a cicada, I'd stay underground."

Murphy said, "They eat them in China."

Sam said, "See."

Murphy said, "Stir-fry."

Sam said, "If we could get some, we could wok them up for my sister."

It was lunch. They were eating at Sam's. Grilled cheese. Carrot sticks. Chocolate milk.

Morley was leaving for work, but she hadn't got out the door yet. She was standing in the middle of the kitchen with her hands on her hips. She was considering something.

"No," she said, "no videos. It's summer. It's a beautiful day. Play outside."

Sam said, "We're bored of outside."

Morley said, "That's funny. I thought you were bored of school. Adam Turlington is going to *summer* school. I bet summer school isn't boring."

Arthur, the dog, was lying in the cool dust under the back steps. Sam was holding a cup, dripping water on him through the slats.

Murphy said, "We should get the hose."

And that, more or less, is the moment it all began.

They called Peter Moore. They said, "Bring your bathing suit. And a sprinkler."

By the middle of the afternoon, there were five boys running around the backyard. Five boys and two sprinklers.

One sprinkler was attached to the garden tap and one was running out the back door, hooked up to the basement sink.

And the middle of the afternoon is when Rashida Chudary came by with little Fatima in tow. Rashida was on her way to the grocery store. She had stopped by with something for Morley. When no one answered the front door, she came around the back.

Fatima got sprayed. She squealed, but it was a squeal of delight. In fact, the tears only came when her mother said they had to go. One thing led to another, and Fatima ended up staying.

"We'll take care of Fatima," said Sam.

And they did—magnificently. They unscrewed one of the sprinklers and replaced it with a nozzle. They set the nozzle to jet spray. They set Fatima on a chair on the back of the deck. They gave her the jet hose. Fatima blasted them with the hose as they ran around the yard.

Fatima stood on her chair, up on her toes, whirling the hose around with the intensity of one of those white-gloved traffic policemen, with their crisply ironed shirts and braids looping over their shoulders. Fatima was in a watery heaven.

It was, beyond a doubt, the most wonderful fun Fatima had had in her entire life—ever. Better than anything. Better than *Eid*.

When Rashida came to get her daughter after an hour, Fatima wouldn't leave.

Sam said, "She can stay. *We'll* bring her home."

When Sam and Murphy did bring Fatima home, Rashida gave them ten dollars.

"Sweet," said Murphy.

It was Murphy's idea to pick Fatima up the next afternoon. But before Sam and Murphy headed off to her place, they spent the morning getting ready. They got Peter Moore to bring his wading pool over. They dragged Sam's old sandbox from a forgotten corner of the yard, and set it in the sun so the sand would dry out. They made lemonade.

Then the three of them walked over to the Chudarys' place and knocked on their door, standing on the stoop like three little Jehovah's Witnesses.

When Rashida answered, it was Murphy who did the talking.

"We were wondering," said Murphy, "if Fatima would like to come to our water park."

On the first day of their water park's operation, they got Fatima and Erik Schmidt's little brother Jürgen. They led Fatima and Jürgen through the sprinklers, let them spray the hoses and watched them splash in the pool. After two hours, Peter walked the soggy and exhausted toddlers home.

Sam and Murphy stayed behind, putting everything back in place and mopping up the basement. They were almost finished when Peter marched into the backyard, with two ten-dollar bills. They had made twenty bucks.

Murphy went to his cottage over the weekend, which didn't really matter because it rained on Saturday. But they were back at it on Monday. Murphy, who had had two days to think about things, arrived with three white T-shirts and two days of pent-up plans.

They set up the backyard: the sandbox, the wading pool and the sprinklers. Then Murphy produced the white T-shirts.

"We should look professional," said Murphy. They put on the white T-shirts and headed off. They were looking for customers.

That afternoon there were seven kids in the backyard. Four of them paying customers.

"Campers," said Murphy. "Not customers."

It's not clear who thought up the waterslide. It *might* have been Fatima. Something about being the first kid there, the founding member of this club or camp or whatever this was—something, anyway, had given the normally shy four-year-old a massive injection of self-assurance. The highlight of each afternoon was the game they now called Jet Stream, the game in which Fatima stood on her chair, and whirled around and around with the hose, making them all run and squeal. Fatima, the smallest by a good half-foot, twisted and turned, running the backyard with the authority of a symphony conductor.

The waterslide could have been Fatima's idea. But no one remembers anymore. And it doesn't really matter.

Old Eugene who lives next door was involved. It wouldn't have happened without Eugene. It wasn't his idea, of course, and no one ever tried to say it was. But he *was* involved. It wouldn't have happened without him.

Eugene had been watching since the water park first began. How could he not? Eugene, in his blue suit pants and his matching vest, the sleeves of his white dress shirt rolled to the elbows, had watched, sitting where he always sits on hot summer afternoons, on the old kitchen chair under his grape arbour. He was smoking one of his Italian cigars, nursing a tumbler of his homemade Chianti, tilting his chair danger-ously backward, his feet feathering the fence whenever he started to teeter.

The day the waterslide was born, Eugene, in the middle of his ninety-second summer, tilted dangerously back in his kitchen chair under the grape arbour, the fruit flies buzzing around him, and the children too. He had been wondering if he should open another bottle of the five-year-old Chianti, or try some of last year's batch, but then he had been taken over with the children and what they were trying to do. What in God's name were they trying to do? They had two slides they had removed from two playsets, and they were duct-taping them together. Or trying to. They seemed to be trying to make them into one long slide.

"Sam," called Eugene, in his throaty whisper, waving his spotted arm in the air. If it was a slide they needed, he had a better one. It was in his shed. He was pretty sure.

"Sam," he called again, coughing and spitting on the ground, gesturing at the shed at the bottom of his garden.

Eugene has one of just about everything down in the shed: gardening tools, household appliances, leftover construction supplies. And that doesn't even scratch the surface. There was also contraband, for instance: hidden bottles of eau-de-vie, secret cases of cigars.

He led the boys around his wife's flower bed, past his famous fig tree, under the grape arbour, between the rows of peppers and tomatoes and into the earthy cool of the shaded shed.

When his watery eyes adjusted to the light, Eugene started Sam, Peter and Murphy moving stuff around: an old refrigerator, a bureau, two hand-push lawn mowers. It was dirty work and they were getting hot and annoyed because they didn't understand what he was up to. Then they unearthed it. Eugene stepped back, and beamed, and the boys stood there in the sticky darkness without saying a word, struck dumb, staring into the back corner of Eugene's shed as if they had just uncovered the gold mask of Tutankhamen. It was the greatest treasure they could imagine—a long plastic tube. It was a portable industrial garbage chute, the kind you use when renovating houses to slide debris from the second floor to the yard. Eugene had packed the chute into the garage thinking someone might have a use for it some day. And now they did.

Sam and Murphy had been trying to build a waterslide that ran from the back deck down to the garden. A little slide. A modest drop. But by the time they had finished, by the time they had heaved Eugene's enormous plastic tube out of the shed, and dropped it over the fence, they had also heaved modesty out the window.

This was the waterside to end *all* waterslides. This waterslide didn't start on the deck. This waterslide began at the second-floor bathroom window, traversed the family-room roof, looped around the clothesline pole, rolled over the picnic table and ended in the back garden near the pear tree.

Fatima stood on the deck with her little arms folded over her chest as the boys worked, nodding occasionally, pointing at this and then at that, like the foreman at a construction site.

It took most of the afternoon to assemble it. The hardest part was connecting the slides from the playsets to Eugene's chute. They finally figured it out, and when they did, they all agreed it just might be the greatest waterslide built. *Ever.*

Any normal adult watching this unfold would have been seized by a spasm of anxiety and put a stop to it. But Eugene was the only adult watching. And at ninety-two, Eugene was a lot closer to boys, and the boyhood call to adventure, than he was to the anxiety levels of any normal adult.

What could possibly go wrong? After two wars and ninety-one and a half summers, the only thing Eugene worried about was his cellar of homemade wine, and the boys' slide wasn't going anywhere near that.

Fatima was the first one down. She bounced to her feet at the bottom like a trapeze artist. She confirmed it—it *was* the greatest waterslide ever built.

Word spread overnight. No one actually *told* anyone. The news spread through the telepathy of childhood. By the next day, there wasn't a boy or a girl in the neighbourhood who didn't know about the waterslide in Dave and Morley's backyard. No *adults* knew about it. The boys disassembled it at the end of the afternoon. They spent the next morning putting it back together. They didn't believe they were doing anything wrong. They just had that intuitive understanding, shared by all children, that there are perfectly innocent things children do that adults are not equipped to handle.

No one was surprised then, the very next afternoon, when about twenty-five kids showed up. Or that everyone knew, without anyone saying anything, to wheel their bikes down the drive and lean them behind the house, so they didn't attract attention from the street.

What did surprise them, however, was the moment that second afternoon when Eugene, who had been watching the children quietly from his chair under the arbour for two days straight, stood up, went inside and came out fifteen minutes later wearing nothing but a bathing cap and a knee-length blue bathing suit. He grinned, and waved at the kids, and then he propped his pruning ladder against the fence and climbed over, the veins on his knotty old legs throbbing with excitement.

It was Chris Turlington who started filming all this on his cellphone. It was his twin sister, Christina, who encouraged other kids to do the same, then edited the footage into a surprisingly slick video and posted it on YouTube.

Dave never would have seen it if he didn't work in a record store and his staff weren't attuned to this sort of stuff. A lot of people, apparently, are attuned. Tens of thousands, actually. *The Waterslide* became the most-watched video about an hour after it was posted. Everyone was talking about it. Though you understand when I say, everyone, I mean everyone of a certain age.

It was the Tuesday, I think. Although it could have been the Wednesday. It's hard to be certain about this. And it's not important. The days tend to blur together at the Vinyl Cafe, especially in the summer.

Anyway, it was the afternoon—that part is for sure. Dave

was by the counter reading out loud from the back of a James Last album.

"Listen to this," he said to Brian, who has worked at the record store for years. "*This is a High Fidelity recording.*" Brian is Dave's oldest employee by far. Dave was reading this to Brian and to one of Brian's friends, who doesn't work at the store, but easily spends as much time there as Brian.

"*It is designed,*" Dave read, "*to play on the phonograph of your choice. If you are the owner of a new stereophonic system, this record will play on it. You can purchase this record with no fear of it becoming obsolete.*"

"What do you think?" said Dave. "Right or wrong?"

"Depends," said Brian.

"On what?" said Dave.

"On whether they're talking about the record as a concept or the concept of James Last."

"What ever happened to James Last?" said Dave.

"Exactly," said Brian.

Brian wandered behind the counter and dropped into the chair in front the computer.

He typed *James Last* into Google. Fifteen minutes passed before Brian was heard from again.

"Oh, oh, oh," said Brian. "Have you seen this?"

Brian had given up on James Last and had flipped on YouTube.

"You have to see this," said Brian.

Dave wandered over and peered at the screen. Brian pressed play.

This is what Dave saw: a grainy and very shaky close-up of an impossibly old man struggling over a fence. Then there was a cut and a jerky shot of the back of a house. The camera pulled back, and Dave saw there were kids dancing on the back roof of this house. Then the shot zoomed in, and Dave saw something that looked like a bobsled run coming out the upstairs window.

There was something familiar about it all. "I think I have seen this before," said Dave. "This is like déjà vu."

Then the camera zoomed in on one of the kids dancing on the roof. The boy had one of those tiny Italian cigars in his mouth.

"I know this place," said Dave. "Is this a frat house? It looks like a frat house."

Dave leaned forward, squinting at the screen. The picture was so fuzzy it was hard to be sure. The camera zeroed in on the window. A small face and two hands appeared. Whoever it was, was holding a bottle in each hand and dumping the contents of the bottle down the slide.

"I think that's detergent," said Brian.

"Shampoo," said Brian's friend. "That's jojoba shampoo."

They all looked at him.

"I recognize the bottle," said Brian's friend.

"Ohmigod," said Dave.

"You ain't seen anything," said Brian. "It gets wicked better."

There was another edit and the camera focused on the old guy again. It was hard to make him out because the kids were gathered around him slapping him on the back. The old guy was doing something to his mouth.

"Ohmigod," said Dave again.

It was Eugene, of course, and Eugene was doing what he always does before he does anything that requires exertion.

He was reaching into his mouth and removing his false teeth.

As Dave watched, the old man handed his teeth to a little girl who was standing on a chair holding a garden hose. The girl held the teeth high in the air. All the kids applauded. Now she was stuffing them into her pocket. She turned her hose onto the slide.

The camera left her to follow the old man inside the house. Up the stairs, into the bathroom.

Dave said, "Is this live?"

There was another edit. The old man was putting on a pair of nose plugs. There was a close-up of the shower. Two young boys were helping the toothless old man up onto the toilet and out the bathroom window. Then the point of view changed and the camera was outside again. It was on the ground, and there was the back of the house and then the camera zoomed in on the bathroom window. Everything was still for a few seconds, until—POW—the impossibly old man came flying out the window. He was sitting down and waving at the camera—until he hit the frothy spot where the boy had poured the jojoba shampoo. When he hit that spot, he flipped onto his back, gaining speed, his feet wiggling in the air. And that's when everything came into focus for poor Dave. The old man, it was, ohmigod, it looked exactly like Eugene from next door.

"I have to go," said Dave.

"It gets better," said Brian. "The whole point is the end. When he hits the garden fence."

But Dave was already out of the store.

So Dave missed the moment when Eugene flew out the bottom of the slide like he'd been shot out of a cannon. And he missed the part where Eugene smacked into the garden fence—the part where the old man struggled to his feet and stood there, toothless, covered with bubbles, his nose plug on, grinning madly, laughing, until he spotted his wife, Maria, on the other side of the fence. When he saw Maria glaring at him, his smile vanished, and his shoulders sagged.

"Busted," said Eugene, sadly, to the camera.

Dave, who was already through the front door, missed that part. He was gone like a shot, turning right, past Dorothy's bookstore, past Kenny Wong's café, thinking *don't stop … there's no time to stop.* He had to get home, he had to…. He got four blocks, four long blocks, but no more, before his poor pounding adrenaline-shot heart felt as if it were going to explode. He pulled up short, gasping for breath. This was ridiculous; he couldn't run all the way home. He needed to get a taxi. He got a taxi.

"Hurry," said Dave. "Hurry." Waving a twenty-dollar bill at the taxi driver.

It was 4:30. The hottest part of the day was done. Sam and Murphy were on the back porch, sitting on the double hammock. Well, they were more slouched than sitting. Or sprawled. Inching back and forth, but barely. The perfect picture of summer indolence. As still as a hot wind on a summer lake.

Dave burst onto this scene like a dog with a fetched ball. Dave was all sweaty and panting and out of breath. Doglike Dave.

Murphy and Sam looked up at him from the hammock with sleepy boredom.

"Hey Dad," said Sam.

"Boys," said Dave.

"Hey," said Sam.

This was not what he had expected at all. This was the last thing he had expected.

He looked over the fence. Eugene was sitting where he always sat—under the grape arbour, tilting back on his kitchen chair, his arm in a sling.

Dave looked at Eugene and then at the boys. He walked over to the fence and nodded. Eugene nodded back and spat on the ground.

Once when he was a boy, Dave's parents gave him a dart set. He had begged them for the dart set. He couldn't remember why. But he wanted it, and they gave it to him for his birthday.

Now in those days, Dave's favourite show on television was *Circus Boy*, a show that chronicled the weekly adventures of a young boy called Corky, whose parents, the Flying Falcons, were killed in a high-wire accident. Corky was adopted by a clown named Joey and rode Bimbo the elephant in the show. He was played by, of all people, Micky Dolenz, later of Monkees fame. (Years later Dave and Dolenz and Mitch Ryder had a wolf of a night in London reminiscing about the TV show.)

The episode that had the biggest impact on Dave was about a knife-thrower and his wife. Dolenz didn't remember it. But Dave did. Dave remembered it vividly. The wife was tied to a board. The assistant put the blindfold on the knife-thrower and spun him in a circle. Dave remembered everything about the show—the way the blindfolded man threw the knives at his wife, the way the knives stuck in the board all around her.

Dave was maybe eight when that show was on the air. He took his little sister, Annie, into the basement, and he stood her against the basement wall, and he threw his new darts at her. The first one stuck in her knee. The second in her shoulder. After the second one, she said, "This is a stupid game," and ran upstairs.

Their mother fainted when she saw the darts sticking out of her daughter. When Dave explained why he had done this thing with the darts, his father seemed to understand, though he did confiscate the dart set. Dave always thought well of his father that he didn't get mad. Or lecture him. It was an accident, and Dave wouldn't have done it again. His father knew that.

Dave smiled at Eugene over the fence.

Dave said, "You okay?"

"Ahh," said Eugene, motioning toward the vegetable patch with his head. "Gardening accident."

Dave said, "Sorry to hear that."

Maria, who was sitting beside her husband, snorted.

Dave nodded and walked back to the boys in the hammock. "What have you boys been up to?"

"We watered the garden," said Sam.

"Front and back?" said Dave. He was looking around. The grass was wet; the bathroom window was closed. There were no children dancing on the roof.

"Just the back," said Sam.

"Looks like you did a good job," said Dave.

Except for a few telltale soap bubbles clinging to the pear tree, everything was in order.

Dave said, "You've probably done enough watering for the next little while."

"Yeah," said Sam. "Probably."

Dave looked at his son hard. Sam looked back, nodding his head.

Sam said, "We are pretty much through with the watering."

Okay, thought Dave, *my move*. He knew it. They knew it. The boys were getting up.

"We are going to the park," said Sam.

Line of least resistance, thought Dave. *Lead me on.*

"That's a good idea," said Dave. He dug into his pocket and pulled out a bill. "Why don't you stop by Lawlor's and get yourself an ice cream."

Sam glanced at Murphy.

Murphy patted his bulging pockets.

"That's okay," said Sam. "We've got money."

Dear Mr. McLean,

My fiancé and I are planning our wedding, and while you don't know us, we are convinced you'd do a great job of MCing the evening. I've included a list of notes about Aaron and myself, but you also should be aware of the following:

Our colour palette is fuchsia and Palermo blue. I trust that you could wear a suit that incorporates the colour scheme.

Please don't mention Aunt Kate's drinking.

The Radcliffes and the Kluskys are not on speaking terms.

Cousin Harold has anger issues.

Please be prepared to cut short Uncle Neal's "toast to the bride" if he begins to ramble.

Thanks so much for considering this. I'm so excited. Aren't weddings fun?

Emma

Dear Emma,

I'm terribly sorry to say that I seem to have a conflict with that date. I am really disappointed not to be part of this celebration. Really.

MARGARET
GETS MARRIED

On the last Saturday in March, a grey and woolly day if ever there was one, Sandy Rutledge, of Rutledge's Hardware Store, on River Street, in Big Narrows, Cape Breton, stayed after everyone else had left for the day so he could organize the hardware store's first-ever window display. Sandy graduated from business school, the first in his family to go to university. Ever since graduation, he had been bugging his father to let him make some changes.

Willard Rutledge finally relented. Sandy stayed late, and by Monday, at lunch, pretty much everyone in town had heard about Rutledge's new front window. People were making special trips just to check it out.

What Sandy did was clean out the mess of doorbells, the bags of birdseed and the towers of toasters and kettles that had accumulated in the front window over the last seventy-four years. He replaced the entire jumble with a solitary mannequin. It, or more to the point, she, was wearing a bridal gown. Sandy picked up the mannequin, and the gown, second-hand from a shop in Sydney. The idea, it being just a few weeks until spring, was to encourage the brides of Big Narrows to register at the hardware store.

By the end of the week, much to Sandy's delight, they had two brides. And a third, Becky Michel, of Fletcher's Harbour, was wavering under pressure from her fiancé, Cliff, who had wanted a nail gun since he was seven.

Dave's mother, Margaret, was one of the last people in town to see the window. Smith Gardner picks Margaret up every Thursday afternoon, and they go to the Elks' meat raffle. After that, they go to the Maple Leaf Restaurant for the all-you-can-eat buffet.

On Thursday, as they pulled in to Kerrigan's parking lot Smith said, "Do you want to see the window?"

Margaret said, "Sure."

As Margaret peered at the wedding dress, Smith said, "I wouldn't want to go through *that* again." Margaret nodded. Then they stood there awkwardly. *That* was the first time Smith and Margaret talked about marriage.

When she got home, Margaret stared in her bathroom mirror.

"Uh-oh," she said.

It was the middle of April by the time Smith decided to propose. He drove to Sydney to get a ring.

His late wife, Jean, had hated her wedding ring. She said it irritated her finger. Eventually she took it off and wore the ring on a chain around her neck.

Smith didn't want Margaret to hate *her* ring. So all he bought was a diamond. The jeweller said they could come back together and choose a setting. It was a modest stone.

"But it has good colour," said the jeweller, holding it up to the light.

Smith dropped the bag with the diamond in it on the passenger seat of his pickup. He pulled off the road as soon as he'd crossed the Seal Island Bridge. He shook the diamond into his rough hand, took a deep breath and held it in the sun. It didn't look like it had any colour to him. It looked as clear as glass.

On his way through town, Smith stopped at Kerrigan's and bought a tub of ice cream—Margaret's favourite flavour, maple walnut. He took the ice cream to Margaret's house for Sunday lunch.

After the sandwich plates had been cleared from the table, Smith got the ice cream from the freezer. He put a generous scoop into Margaret's bowl, set the diamond on top of the ice cream and set the bowl in front of her. He sat waiting, his heart pounding as she picked up her spoon.

Margaret polished off the entire bowl and sat back.

"That was good," she said.

Not knowing what to say, Smith didn't say anything. He drove to Sydney the next morning.

"I want *another* diamond," he said to the jeweller. "A *bigger* one. With more colour. So it stands out."

The jeweller put a velvet tray on the counter and showed him the stones.

"That one," said Smith. "But this time put it in a ring."

"What kind of setting?" asked the jeweller.

"A comfortable one," said Smith.

"What size?" asked the jeweller.

"Medium," said Smith.

The first warm weekend in May, Margaret and Smith went to Ignish to visit Smith's son. On the way home Smith said, "Let's go back the long way. Through the Bay."

Irish Bay. Where Margaret grew up.

Margaret almost said, *It's getting late.* Instead she said, "That would be nice, Smith."

They pulled off the highway at the gas station and came into town at the south end, past the Stinsons' farm and Dr. Sandberg's old place. It had been dark for an hour when Smith pulled up in front of the house where she was born.

Margaret said, "So long ago."

Smith said, "Let's see if the irises are up."

Margaret felt anxious. She didn't know the people who lived there anymore. City people. But Smith was already walking around the front of his pickup.

Smith said, "There is no one home. Just a peek."

Against her better instincts, Margaret followed Smith across the damp lawn, the dew chilly on her feet. She was nervous, but she was also intrigued. She heard a click as he slid the gate latch in the darkness, and she followed him into the yard. The yard where she and Elizabeth had played when they were girls.

It was so strange to be there again. She smiled at Smith and then she turned to go. She was nervous to stay too long. Smith didn't move.

Slipping a ring on Margaret's finger, under the moon, in the garden where she had been a girl and had probably dreamt of such things, had seemed like such a good idea. In the abstract. But here in the garden, it didn't seem like a good idea at all.

Smith was feeling light-headed and woozy. His legs were shaking.

"Smith?" said Margaret.

Smith had slipped the ring out of his pocket. He lurched forward and grabbed Margaret's hand.

Margaret, who couldn't see the ring in the darkness, could sense Smith's unsteadiness. But it was his face that gave him away. It was written on his face. It was as clear as day. Smith was about to tell her that he was sick, dying probably.

"Oh Smith," she said. "No."

"No?" said Smith. "I haven't even asked yet."

And that's when Margaret glanced down and saw the ring for the first time. She started to laugh.

Smith had gone over this moment many times in his mind. He had imagined many responses. But never ... laughter. He didn't see what was so damn funny.

Margaret said, "Oh Smith." But before she could say anything else, a light flicked on upstairs, and a window banged opened. Smith swore. And he tugged Margaret's hand. Smith and Margaret ran out of the back garden and tumbled into his truck like a pair of teenagers. They ripped down the street, around the corner and all the way to the church before they stopped.

"My heart," said Smith, resting his head on the wheel.

Margaret waited for him to settle.

When he did, Margaret said, "Smith Gardner. Did you just ask me to marry you?"

Smith didn't lift his head. "Yes," he said. "Did you just refuse?"

Margaret said, "No, Smith."

"The ring goes on the *left* hand, Smith," she said.

Then she added, "Good Lord."

Smith was so overtaken with the moment that he had forgotten he was driving. They were drifting through the intersection, heading right for the Carruthers' front lawn.

The ring was too big. They took it back to the jeweller to have it sized. They picked it up a week later. On the way out of the store, Margaret stopped, took it off her finger and slipped it into her purse.

Smith said, "Why did you do that?"

Margaret said, "Smith, people are going to see it if I keep it on my hand."

Smith said, "We certainly wouldn't want that."

For a week Margaret didn't tell a soul. She fretted instead. The truth was the whole thing embarrassed her. In her heart she wished that she and Smith could do what the young kids did and move in together.

After a week of fretting, she picked up the telephone. It was a Sunday afternoon. Smith had already told *his* kids. She couldn't delay any longer. She had to phone her daughter, Annie, in Halifax.

And David.

"Hi," she said. "How are things?"

She had been working in the garden. She was wearing her gardening slacks and an oversized cardigan that used to belong to her late husband, Charlie. She was standing by the kitchen window. Her hands still had dirt on them. She had called her son first. Her eldest.

She took a deep breath. She said, "David, I have something to tell you."

"You're sick," said Dave.

"Worse," said Margaret. "Smith asked me to marry him."

Dave shouldn't have been so surprised. He knew that this was coming. Smith had as good as asked his permission that afternoon in the graveyard. When was that, anyway?

He shouldn't have been surprised. But he was. So when Margaret blurted it out, Dave was *not* his best self.

Margaret said, "Smith asked me to marry him," and the first thing Dave said was "Where will you be buried, then? There is supposed to be a space beside Dad."

Margaret said, "I honestly hadn't considered that."

Dave was as amazed as she was at what had just come out of his mouth.

He said, "I suppose the fact that it doesn't really matter to me where you're buried won't stop you from telling everyone that that was my reaction."

Margaret said, "Probably not."

Dave said, "Well congratulations, anyway. He's a nice guy. I mean, I think he is a wonderful guy. I'm happy." He should have left it there, but he kept going; he added, "For you."

Dave didn't really want to talk about it, which was fine because neither did she. They talked about her garden instead. And then they said goodbye.

When Margaret hung up, she shrugged. It was the first time she had said it out loud. *I am getting married.*

"That wasn't so bad," she said. She waited five minutes before she phoned Annie.

"Ohmigod," said Annie. "Where will you be buried?"

There was a stunned silence and then Margaret said, "David called you." And Annie snorted, and they both laughed and laughed. When they stopped laughing, Annie said, "Oh Mom, I am so happy for you. How did he ask?"

And Margaret said, "He asked me under the moon in the garden in Irish Bay."

And Annie said, "I want to know every last detail."

Now that she had spoken the words out loud, Margaret figured she might as well keep going.

The next morning, she went to Kerrigan's grocery store knowing she would bump into Winnie. Winnie always shopped Monday mornings. They met in front of the lunch meats. Margaret took a deep breath and said, offhandedly, "We're thinking about having the reception at the Curling Club."

Winnie said, "What reception?"

Margaret said, "Didn't I tell you?"

Everyone in town knew by lunch. It didn't go as badly as Margaret had imagined.

It went worse than she had imagined.

When you are eighty-four years old, you don't want people treating you as if you're cute. Everyone thought it was cute. Everyone thought it was sweet.

"It makes me wish you had some sort of problem," she said to Smith as they walked his dog along the road behind Macaulays' farm. "Couldn't you start drinking or something?"

And that was before Bernadette and Winnie were warmed up. That was before Bernadette and Winnie started on about what Margaret should wear.

Margaret has never fussed about fashion. You live in a place like the Narrows, and the best way to dress is to dress for chores. Which is more or less how Margaret dresses. Margaret's favourite clothes are sweaters. Her favourite accessory is a rake.

"I don't want it to be a big fancy thing," said Margaret.

"I am not advising a floor-length gown," said Winnie. Bernadette nodded in agreement. "In fact," said Winnie, "I would advise against it. You need a proper dress and a jacket. I know a lady in Halifax who does a lovely job with seed pearls."

They were at the post office, in front of the mailboxes. While Winnie was talking, Bernadette had pulled a tape measure out of her purse. Before Margaret knew what was happening, Bernadette was wrapping it around her middle.

"We are not," said Margaret, pulling the tape measure from her waist, "going to Halifax."

There is nothing like a wedding to addle people's minds. Especially, it turns out, if those people have spent too many of their recent years planning funerals.

As April opened into May, everyone in Big Narrows, everyone of a certain age, that is, was fussing over the first big celebration that had come their way for decades.

Margaret-Anne Madigan, for instance, who had organized five weddings in her life, and had gotten pretty good at it before the opportunities dried up, phoned Margaret as soon as she heard the news.

"First thing," she said, barely saying hello, "book the hair appointments. Make sure there is more than one stylist for you and your bridesmaids. You don't want to be there all day."

"Bridesmaids?" said Margaret doubtfully.

"Then call the florist." Margaret-Anne was on a roll. In the *Reader's Digest*, she had read about a hybrid rose named after Diana, the Princess of Wales.

"It has a beautiful scent," said Margaret-Anne, who had never actually seen one, let alone smelled one. "Sweet and fruity. You can get them flown up from Boston. Just tell them your colour palette."

And it wasn't just the women. The men may not have been taken up with flowers and dresses, but they still found plenty to fuss about. Alex Cunningham cornered Margaret at the Maple Leaf Restaurant.

"I've been thinking I'd be hearing from you, Margaret," said Alex.

Alex ran the Elks Lodge. And as far as Alex was concerned, the Elks Lodge was the only place in the Narrows where a woman of distinction would consider holding her wedding reception.

Of course the Reverend Wright thought the same thing about the Church Hall.

As did all Smith's friends at the Legion. *They* deputized George MacDonnell to speak on their behalf.

George ambushed her in the parking lot at Kerrigan's. "We best be nailing down the reception," said George. "There are lots of other events that month. The sausage festival is on the twelfth, you know."

"Have you been to booking the music now, Margaret?"

asked Alf MacDonald when he zeroed in on her in front of the library.

Alf's son Sid, who deejayed at a hip-hop club in Yarmouth, was going to be in Halifax the week of the wedding.

"He's getting his tattoo worked on," said Alf.

Sid had been adding to his art as he could afford it. When it was finished, his tattoo would cover his entire body and tell the life story of Celine Dion, with the lavish Vegas wedding scene covering most of his back.

"Sid could slip back here you know. I doubt he has ever done a wedding, but he has good gear."

Margaret began to dread going out. Wherever she went, there was someone hovering with some sort of unwanted advice. She didn't leave her house for three days.

Somewhere in there she phoned Annie.

She said, "I think I am going to call it off. I don't think I can stand the pressure."

Of all people, Margaret thought Annie would understand. That Annie would be on her side.

But Annie was no different from the rest of them. It was like she hadn't heard a word Margaret had said. Margaret says she is going to call the whole thing off and Annie says, "Have you settled the menu yet? You have to make sure you have a vegetarian option. Don't forget Margot is vegan now."

Margaret sighed. She said, "Vegan. That means she eats chicken, right?"

On her fourth day of self-imposed exile, she phoned Smith.

"I can't do this," she said. "We can't get married."

She expected he would come over and try to talk her out of it. Or, more to the point, into it. He didn't. Instead he said, "That's okay. I understand."

That night she went up to the attic with a box of winter stuff. She wasn't planning on bringing any summer stuff down, but once she got there she began poking around. She wasn't looking for anything, nothing important. When she climbed into the far corner, she came face to face with Charlie's uniform from the war. It was hanging on a post. It was wrapped in a plastic dry cleaner's bag. According to the tag, it had last been cleaned in April 1963. There was a shoebox beside it. She knew what was in it. It was filled with letters that Charlie had written her from England. She flicked on an old lamp and sat in its orange glow for the longest time, reading those letters.

Dear one. We arrived here at 7 p.m. and I half-thought there might be a wire. It's absurd to think I have only been away for a week.

Her eyes flicked to the bottom of the page.

Now my dearest love, I must say goodnight. It is nearly twelve. God bless you, my dear, dear girl.

There was a box of photo albums somewhere. When she finished the letters, she took the first album and settled it in her lap. Pictures of the kids. David, maybe five years old. And there was their first car. It looked so ancient. She ran her finger across the page as if she could reach back through time. As if she could touch the past by touching the little black and white photos, with their serrated edges. There were titles under each picture, printed on the black paper with white ink in Charlie's hand. *Annie at the beach. Hungry Dave. Bath time.*

She opened the next book. It was her wedding pictures.

She slammed it shut. She stood up and started for the stairs. Then she took a deep breath and sat down and opened the book again.

It was well past midnight when she left the attic.

A day and a half more went by before she called Smith back.

"I was getting worried," said Smith.

"I'm sorry," she said.

"That's okay," he said. "No apology necessary. It's pretty crazy out there."

Then she said, "I am coming over for dinner, day after tomorrow. I'll be bringing someone with me."

That afternoon, she drove to town and parked in front of Arnie Gallagher's storefront. As well as being the duly elected mayor of Big Narrows, Arnie Gallagher runs the town's only flower shop, travel agency, gift depot, bait store and funeral home—all from his storefront on Water Street.

Margaret walked in the front door, around the counter and into the back room where Arnie was sitting by an empty casket, packing leeches into plastic foam cups.

"Arnie Gallagher," said Margaret. "Isn't it about time you diversified?"

It was Arnie who Margaret was bringing with her to Smith's for dinner.

Arnie spent the day in Sydney getting himself ready.

They arrived together in Arnie's truck. Margaret let herself in through the back door.

"Meet our new wedding planner," she said to Smith.

Arnie dropped a big book on Smith's kitchen table.

"First things first," he said. "First you've got to choose the invitation."

"Why we would be delighted, Arnie," said Margaret. Then she pointed at a stain on the cover.

"Arnie Gallagher," said Margaret. "I do believe you have got some leech guts on your invitation book already."

Arnie pulled a red handkerchief out of his jean jacket and dabbed at the book. "*Hope* that's leech," said Arnie.

It took them an hour and a half. After an hour and a half, they had settled everything.

Arnie stayed for supper.

It was smooth sailing after that. From then on if anyone tried to talk to her, Margaret told them to talk to Arnie.

"Arnie's in charge," she said.

Margaret showed up at Smith's house again first thing the next morning.

She was carrying a pile of books in her arms. She dropped them on the kitchen table. The photo albums.

"Sit down," she said. "I am going to tell you everything about me."

And that is what they did. They sat in the kitchen and she told him the story of her life. He already knew most of it, but he had never heard it all in one piece like that—from the very beginning to the end. They looked at the pictures. They read the old letters from Charlie. When she was finished she said, "Now you know everything. Now I have no secrets from you. You know it all from beginning to end."

"Not quite to the end," said Smith. "There's still a bit left."

They were married on July the tenth. There was only a small group at the ceremony. But most of the town came to the reception. Many of them were kids she had taught. They held the reception in the school gym. That was Smith's idea.

Bernadette baked the cake. Smith's son toasted the groom. And Dave gave the toast to the bride. He said the nicest things. "My mother," he began, "has always lived in a state of grace. Many people go through their entire life without ever finding true love. She has found it twice."

Oh. The dress.

That was the only battle Arnie *didn't* win.

Margaret wandered into Gallagher's one afternoon and found Arnie backed up against the bait fridge, Winnie and Bernadette standing in front of him waving their arms and stamping their feet.

So two weeks before the wedding, Margaret finally agreed to go shopping in Halifax. She got an ivory suit from the lady who did the pearl detailing.

Winnie said it was perfect. Bernadette agreed. Margaret thought otherwise. "It makes me look like one of those real estate ladies from the city," she said to Dave one night when he phoned.

"I am sure you look just fine," said Dave.

He was right. She did look fine. But she never liked it. And so, that Saturday, on their way to the church, as they were driving down River Street, Margaret turned to Dave, who was driving her, and said, "Pull in there. And park."

Dave glanced at his wristwatch.

Margaret frowned at him and said, "You don't think they'll start without us, do you David?"

Dave knew better than to answer that. He parked Smith's truck, which he was driving, and followed her into Rutledge's Hardware without a word.

Margaret had said she didn't want any gifts. It was Smith's idea that they register at the hardware store. All the things on their list were going to go to a young couple from Little Narrows who had lost everything in a fire.

Margaret winked at Dave as they marched up to the counter together.

"Sandy Rutledge," he heard her say, "how much for that wedding dress in the window?"

She paid twenty-nine dollars for the dress. Tax in. She changed in the staff washroom. They were in and out of the hardware store in under fifteen minutes.

When they pulled up to the church, Dave put his hand on his mother's arm and stopped her from getting out of the car. He smiled at her and he said, "I am happy for you."

She said, "Me too."

Smith threw his head back and laughed when he saw Margaret in the dress. He was beaming as she walked down the aisle on Dave's elbow.

Winnie and Bernadette were horrified. But they got over it. How could they not? Margaret looked radiant.

Winnie and Bernadette had chosen her an outfit for the reception, but Margaret never changed. She wore her hardware bridal gown all night long.

She barely left the dance floor. Margaret danced with all the young men she had taught all those years ago, and she danced with Dave, and Sam, and Arnie Gallagher, and Rodney MacDonnell. She even danced with Smith, who told her, when they had finished dancing, that he loved her dearly but that that would be the last time he would ever dance with her.

"Or anyone," he added. "Never again," he whispered in her ear.

She just laughed and kissed him on the cheek and whispered, "We'll see about that," as he left the dance floor chuckling.

She danced the night away. It was her wedding after all. She had already had for better or for worse, for richer and for poorer, in sickness and in health. This was the part she had given up on. This was happily ever after.

Dear Stuart McLean,

Congratulations! You have just won an all-expenses-paid* trip on our premier holiday cruise line. Fill out the following acceptance form (please include the personal information requested, your social insurance number and current credit-card numbers), and you could find yourself cruising through the Caribbean on our famed luxury liner, the S.S. Credulous, absolutely free of charge. *

Bon Voyage!
Hook and Line Luxury Holidays

*EXCLUDES ANY AIRFARE, CRUISE-TICKET PRICE, FOOD AND BEVERAGE EXPENSES AND TOWEL RENTALS.

Dear H & L,

Yahoo. Count me in.

THE CRUISE

Morley's mother, Helen, comes to dinner most Sundays. Helen is frail enough now that she is happier following her routines than her reflexes. On Sundays, she goes to church in the morning and in the afternoon waits for Morley to come by and pick her up. Morley picks her up. Dave drives her home.

Helen hasn't driven *herself* for three, maybe four years. She still has her Buick. It's in the garage. The gas tank is topped, the plates are up to date and the insurance is paid in full. Helen pays the insurance every fall. She doesn't use the car, but she talks about it as if she does.

Morley will call and say, "I'm on my way," and Helen will say, "Why don't *I* just drive down; it would be so much easier."

Helen *never* drives down. Morley always gets her. And Dave always takes her home. That's the routine.

It makes Morley crazy that her mother still pays the insurance.

"What's the point of that?" she says.

"Who cares?" says Dave "The *point* is, she isn't driving. You *say* something, she'll *start* driving to prove you're wrong. The *point* is, you let sleeping dogs lie."

Helen still manages, as they say, still gets about. Church on Sunday. Bridge on Tuesday afternoons. She still cooks, and her house is more or less clean. Not the way it used to be, but it used to be so clean it made Morley crazy.

There is no doubt, however, that Helen's world is getting smaller. She had a fall. And sometimes she gets confused. One Sunday, for instance, Morley picked her up and Helen met her at the door holding a flyer from a local pizza joint.

"It came in the mail," said Helen. Helen was agitated, upset about the flyer.

"I don't eat pizza," said Helen. "I don't know why they would send it to me. Do I have to pay it?"

Helen and Roy used to go to Florida every winter. They had a trailer at Clearwater.

"Mobile home," Helen would tell you. "Not trailer. Mobile home."

Whatever you want to call it, they sold it, years ago, when Roy got sick.

When Roy died, Helen and Peggy Whiteside started going on bus trips together: The Wonders of the West, Autumn in Vermont. And then Peggy Whiteside died.

Helen, God bless her, kept travelling. She had always wanted to see Italy. She had the time of her life. And so every autumn for five years, Helen went on an adventure. She followed the footsteps of the Apostles through Turkey, did the vineyards of the Rhone Valley.

Then she signed up for her first-ever cruise. She invited her sister Loretta to come with her. But Loretta broke her hip, and Helen seemed to lose her will.

"I'm tired," she said to Morley. "I've seen enough."

The travel agent told Helen *he* couldn't give her money back, but *she* could give her tickets away.

"You go," she said to Morley and Dave one Sunday night. "You use my tickets."

They tried to convince her otherwise, but she wasn't buying it.

"I'm tired," she said. "I've seen enough."

"A cruise?" said Dave.

They were sitting in the kitchen, the two of them, the lights low, Billie Holiday singing softly in the background.

"It might be nice," said Morley. "You know, sunsets at sea, dancing on the deck, dinner with the captain."

She would have to buy some cruise clothes, of course. Things that would blow in the wind—a flowing skirt, sage green, and a silk dress, a knee-length cream silk dress with flowers. And a big leather tote bag to carry her books and lotions. That would be posh. Morley was sitting at the table with Dave, but she was lost on Planet Shopping.

Dave said, "I don't want to go on a cruise. Bad things happen at sea."

Morley said, "Get over it."

On their way to bed she said, "Do you think she's still okay? Living alone?"

Dave said, "Who?"

Morley said, "My mother."

And so, barely a month later, Dave found himself sitting glumly in the back of an airport taxi heading north on the

I-95, on his way from the Miami International Airport to Port
Everglades, Florida, Terminal 19, the third-largest cruise-ship
terminal in the world. It was noon. *The Empress of Kumar* was
set to sail at dinner. Ten days to some of the most remote
and unknown islands of the Caribbean: Cumanna, famous for
the leatherback turtles that nest on its south beaches; Aqua
de Perico, where you can see remnants of Aztec ruins; and
Santa Madeira, nine hundred acres of arid and treeless
limestone, renowned for the highly endangered Santa
Madeira woodpecker.

The taxi dropped them at the bottom of the gangplank.
They stood on the wharf with their suitcases beside them,
staring up at the boat like a pair of refugees. Dave said, "I
thought it would be bigger."

Morley said, "Don't start."

Dave said, "No really, I thought these boats were huge."

Morley had already picked up her bag and was making her
way on board.

The man at the table in the blue pants and the white shirt
beamed at them and stuck out his hand. His gold name tag
said, "Derek."

"I'm Derek," he said. "Activities director. You must be Morley."

"Actually," said Dave. "She's Morley."

"Silly me," said Derek taking their passports. He handed
Dave an envelope with a key.

"Water view," he said. Then he said, "Captain Harrison plans
on leaving at six."

There was a sign beside the table that said, *Welcome on
Board.* Dave and Morley stood beside the sign, self-

consciously, and Derek took their picture. While he was squinting at the camera, Dave said, "Is the captain's name really Harrison?"

Derek peered at Dave over the flash. "What?" he said.

Dave said, "Captain Harrison? That was Leslie Nielsen's role in *The Poseidon Adventure*."

It turned out water *view* meant water*line*. Their room was a tiny cabin two levels below the deck, with a solitary porthole licked by the ocean. There was a desk, a cupboard, a toilet, but less room than a college dorm. Dave was lying on his bed, the top bunk, Morley was unpacking, when the announcement for dinner came.

"Kind of early, don't you think?" said Dave, looking at his watch. It was only 5:30.

"First night? Maybe?" said Morley.

They headed for the dining room.

"Table twenty-three," said Morley.

They had to wait while a woman with a cane struggled up the stairs in front of them. When they found table twenty-three, a man was there already. He was slumped in a wheelchair. He appeared to be asleep.

"Should I wake him?" said Morley. Dave didn't hear her. He was looking around the room.

"Uh-oh," said Dave.

Morley followed his arm around the room.

"Oh dear," she said.

They were the youngest in the room, by at least a generation. Maybe two.

"Seniors' cruise," said Dave. And that is when their wheel-chair companion jerked alert.

"WHAT ARE YOU DOING AT MY TABLE?" he barked.

After dinner, Dave and Morley went on deck and watched the sun set and the sea turn dark and thick. There wasn't another soul around. They leaned on the railing, listening to the distant thump of the engine.

"Pretty," said Morley, pointing at the first stars.

"How about champagne?" said Dave.

He went inside to get them each a drink.

Derek was locking up the bar.

"Closes at eight, Morley," said Derek.

"It's Dave," said Dave. "Morley was her mother's maiden name."

They were back on deck the next morning. Morley settled in to a shady corner with a pile of magazines. There was still no one around.

It was a little spooky.

"Where is everyone?" she said.

Dave was standing in the sun, leaning against the ship's railing, the warm wind in his hair, his arms stretched out in both directions. He squinted at his wife and shrugged. "Ship of the damned," he said.

Then he said, "I'm going exploring."

He was gone for maybe an hour. When he came back, he had changed into a T-shirt and a pair of cargo shorts.

"There is a video on in the back lounge," he said. "*Birds of the Caribbean.*"

Morley raised herself on her elbow and pointed at the flat blue ocean.

"They're watching videos?" she said.

"Actually," said Dave. "Most of them are asleep."

Dave went downstairs again at 11:30 to fetch sunscreen. There was a lineup at the dining-room door: men in shorts and sandals and knee-length black socks; women in oversized sunglasses carrying large purses.

"Lunch isn't for half an hour," said Dave as he handed Morley the sunscreen. "Do you think they know something we don't?"

Their table companion from the night before, the man in the wheelchair, was polishing off his dessert when Dave and Morley arrived at 12:15.

"YOU'RE LATE," he said.

"Dad," said the woman sitting beside him, "don't be rude."

The woman looked up at them apprehensively. Then back at the man in the wheelchair. She couldn't seem to make up her mind whom she should deal with. She solved the problem by laying her hand on the man's arm and turning to Dave and Morley.

"I'm so sorry," she said. "He's grumpy because I didn't let him have onions on his burger."

"I'VE EATEN ONIONS ALL MY LIFE," said the man in the wheelchair. He poked at the burger on his plate with his long finger. As if it might be alive. As if it might move.

"They're hard on your stomach, Dad," said the woman.

Then she said, "I'm so sorry. I'm Kathy. This is my father. You must be Morley."

"Actually, I'm Dave," said Dave.

The man in the wheelchair said, "SOMETIMES, IN THE WAR, ALL WE HAD WAS ONIONS."

The sea started to roll that afternoon. Not too terribly much, not waves even, just a swell. But it was enough of a swell that you had to reach for the railing every now and then.

Morley was lying by the pool. Dave was wandering around, looking for peanuts or something to munch on, and to see, as he had said to Morley, if he could "spot anyone remotely our age." He had been gone for over an hour, when he came up behind her quietly, reached out and dropped a chocolate bar on her tummy and himself onto the chaise longue beside her.

"It's a lockdown," he said.

Morley pushed herself up on an elbow, picked up the chocolate bar and wrinkled her nose. "What are you talking about?" she said.

She pitched the chocolate bar back to Dave. Dave caught it, smiled and began to unwrap it.

"I met a couple from Alaska. They were coming back from the fitness centre. Deirdre has everything under lock and key. The rock wall is roped off. The hot tub is lukewarm. The treadmills are pre-set on stroll."

Morley said, "Who's Deirdre?"

Dave said, "That nice man who took our photo."

Morley said, "You mean Derek."

Dave said, "Silly me. The poker chips have all been put away. It is twenty-four-hour euchre."

The weather turned. They were in their cabin, lying on their bunks, out of the wind. It wasn't exactly cold on deck—just grey and unpleasant.

Morley said, "Kathy gave her father the cruise for his birthday. She is so patient with him. It makes me feel guilty. Like I should have brought *my* mother."

Dave said, "It's time for supper. We should go."

Morley said, "I don't really feel like eating."

There was no question the sea had turned. The dining room was only half full, but Kathy and her father were both at the table.

"I'm not feeling so good," said Morley.

"I'm not doing so well either," said Kathy.

"THIS IS NOTHING," said the old man, twisting around in his chair, beckoning to the waiter, pointing at his wineglass.

Kathy shook her head when the waiter arrived with the wine. "Just one glass, Dad. It makes you confused."

"YOU'RE THE CONFUSED ONE. YOU SHOULD HAVE SEEN WHAT WE DRANK IN THE WAR."

The weather took a turn for the worse.

Neither Kathy nor Morley made it to lunch the next day.

"NAME'S ... BRUCE ..." said the man in the wheelchair. "BRUCE ... TOWLER."

Between every second word, Bruce paused to catch his breath, looking down at his plate and pushing at his food.

He had three glasses of wine. Dave wasn't about to say no.

He was a dentist.

"USED ... TO BE ... ANYWAY."

He dozed off between the main course and dessert, but he didn't seem at all confused. He snapped awake when the waiter tried to take his dessert away.

"HEY!" he said.

When the meal was finished, a porter came to push Bruce back to his room.

Dave said, "Do you want to go on deck instead?"

Dave pushed Bruce Towler out to the forward deck and the two of them watched the rolling sea. There was no doubt it was getting rockier. Rockier and rockier.

Dave said, "I should check on my wife."

"DOESN'T ... BOTHER ... ME ... A ... BIT," yelled Bruce into the wind.

Dave wasn't sure if he meant the weather or the fact Dave was leaving him.

Morley wasn't doing well.

"I threw up," she said.

Dave sat beside her and stroked her hair. After about an hour, the boat changed course. And when it did, it began a whole new and nastier motion. Pretty soon the ship was being tossed around like a toy boat in a bathtub. Dave felt as if he were inside a giant washing machine.

Before long, the closet door in Dave and Morley's tiny room was slapping open and shut. The drawers in their bureau were banging back and forth. When Morley got up to make a dash to the washroom, her mattress slid off the bunk. When she returned, she lay down on the floor groaning.

"I am not moving," she said.

And that's when Dave remembered Bruce Towler.

"Ohmigod," he said.

It was so rocky Dave could barely walk down the corridor. At one point the ship lurched dramatically, and Dave was actually walking along the starboard wall. A moment later, it lurched to the other side, and he was walking along the port side.

When he got to the lounge, there were people stretched out on the couches. Others were sitting grimly, with their heads between their knees, clutching little white bags to their faces.

Dave peered out the far window at the deck where he had left his lunch partner. Nothing. Then the ship pitched to the port side and a wheelchair flew past the window. A moment later the chair flew by the other way. Bruce Towler was sitting in the wheelchair with his hands above his head, like a kid on a roller coaster. From port to starboard, from starboard to port. He was soaked when Dave fetched him, but he was beaming.

"HAVEN'T ... HAD ... THAT MUCH FUN ... SINCE MY WIFE'S WAKE!"

That was the night Dave met Doris Schick. They literally bumped into each other in the corridor outside the dining room. Dave was heading back to his cabin.

"I'm looking for a card game," said Doris.

You either get seasick or you don't. And Doris, apparently, was missing the seasick gene.

Dave looked in on Morley. She was still on the floor of their cabin. In the fetal position.

"Don't talk to me," she moaned.

And so Dave, who was feeling surprisingly well, and Doris, who had never felt better, retreated to the forward lounge.

Bruce Towler was sitting in the corner. As soon as they sat down, Doris pulled a pewter flask out of her purse.

"Macallan's," she said.

Bruce smiled and held out his hand.

Doris pulled out a deck of cards and began dealing. "Texas Hold'em?" she asked.

And so while dishes crashed around them and most everyone was huddled over motion sickness bags, Dave, Doris, Bruce and an eighty-six-year-old millwright from Seattle sipped fifteen-year-old whisky and played poker until midnight.

Doris, it turned out, used to live in a seniors' residence in Fargo, North Dakota. When she turned eighty-three, she took a hard look at her finances and realized she couldn't afford to stay there for as long as she planned to live. She had been cruising full-time ever since.

"It's cheaper," she said, fanning her hand on the table in front of her. "Food's better." She pointed out at the angry grey sea. "Weather too, mostly."

At 12:30, Dave said, "My wife is below. I should check on her."

"Ahh," said Doris. "Young love. I lost my husband."

"I'm sorry," said Dave.

"It was a long time ago," said Doris.

The skies cleared the next afternoon.

"TOO BAD," said Bruce Towler, waving his hands over his head weakly, "that was fun."

That was the afternoon Dave found a pile of brochures that had spilled out of a drawer in the bar during the worst of the storm: They were about bungee jumping, parasailing and scuba diving.

When Dave asked, Derek rolled his eyes. "We can't run those activities with a crowd like this. Can you imagine?"

Some people say genius is the ability to concentrate with more intensity than the average person. Others say a genius is someone who has the ability to understand complex problems and to use his imagination to solve them. There are those, however, who believe geniuses are people who look at the world with a sense of wonder, and who possess the ability to see things in a fresh, childlike way.

"YOU'RE A BLOODY GENIUS," said Bruce Towler to Dave two hours later.

"DORIS," he shouted, "ARE YOU COMING? WE'RE GOING OVER THE WALL."

Half an hour later Bruce was standing on the upper deck. Well, standing is an exaggeration. He was sort of standing. He was clutching his walker with one hand and the shoulder of a Filipino crew member with the other. A second crew member was strapping him into a nylon harness. Bruce Towler was beaming.

"MAKE SURE YOU GET A GOOD ONE," he said, pointing at Doris Schick. Doris was standing in front of him with her Polaroid camera.

When you are eighty-seven years old, and you can't stand

up anymore without someone standing beside you, when all the movement you can manage is unsteady, when your body has quit on you, but your spirit hasn't, bungee jumping might just be the perfect sport.

The Filipino mate cinched the final strap on Bruce Towler's harness.

"There is nothing to be afraid of, sir," he said.

Bruce Towler squinted at him. "DAMN RIGHT," said Bruce.

The mate was about to say something else. But he was too late. Bruce Towler was already gone. Bruce took a lurching step and flew out over the edge of the ship. Face down and fractious, Bruce Towler was hurtling toward the blue ocean. For the first time in years, he felt as light as air.

"WHOOPEE," he bellowed as he felt the unfamiliar surge of adrenaline racing through him.

It was only when Bruce got to the end of the line and began his bouncing ascent that Dave noticed that Bruce, in his tweed suit and tie, was still clutching his walker. As he yo-yoed by the crowd on the deck, he was waving it over his head.

"WHOOPEE."

Derek, the activities director, arrived at the lifeboats just as Bruce headed over the rails. As Bruce bounced up and down, Derek stood there, his one hand resting on a ring buoy. He was clutching his heart with the other. He looked apoplectic.

Morley resurfaced the next morning. She set herself up again, with her magazines and bag of supplies, by the aft-deck pool.

Dave didn't have time to read by the pool. Dave had cards with Doris at nine, coffee with Bruce at ten-thirty and a shuffleboard playdown at eleven.

"I'll meet you at lunch," Dave told Morley.

When Morley walked into the dining room, Dave was working on dessert.

"I waited," he said. "I thought you weren't coming."

Morley glanced at her wrist. It was ten past twelve.

She stood by the table awkwardly. There were no empty places. Doris Schick was sitting in Morley's seat. Doris smiled up at Morley. She reached out and rested her hand on Dave's arm. "This dear man has been telling me the most wonderful stories." Then she ran her hand through Dave's hair and added, "I lost my husband."

"That is so awful," said Morley. "I am so sorry. When did he die?"

Doris rolled her eyes. "I didn't say he died, dear."

And so the days rolled by.

The weather turned. For the rest of the trip, they were blessed with hot days and long warm nights. The cruise ship stopped at a different island each morning. The lineups to disembark began at least an hour before they arrived.

They all missed the turtles at Cummana. Much the same at Aqua de Perico, where there wasn't time for a side trip to the Aztec ruins.

Many of them, however, did get to see the endangered Santa Madeira woodpecker. It cost five dollars American to enter the tent where it was kept, and an additional seventy-five cents for a cup of pellets if you wanted to feed it. Dave didn't go himself, but Bruce Towler told him the bird was either asleep or stuffed—in any case, not remotely interested in the pellets.

"THEY AREN'T BAD," said Bruce, holding out a cupful and munching away.

By the end of it, Derek, who had been upstaged during the storm, mortified during the bungee jumping and humbled on the shuffleboard court, gave up the ghost. He had lost the crowd, and he knew it. He cancelled the last night's bingo and more or less vanished, his activities schedule in tatters.

And so it was Dave who organized the party on the final night. Well, not exactly party. It was more ... an event. It began on the final afternoon. Bruce Towler had been wheeling along the deck, looking for excitement, when he almost ran Dave over.

"OUT OF MY WAY," he bellowed, picking up momentum.

"Hey," said Dave, laughing. "What's your top speed?"

Just then, Robert James, a ninety-three-year-old retired real estate agent from Boca Raton wheeled into view from the other direction.

"Robert," shouted Dave, "can you go faster than this old codger?"

And that's all it took really. The race was set for 8:30. On the promenade deck. Doris was given the task of spreading the word—discreetly, only to sympathetic passengers.

"Don't let Derek catch wind," said Dave.

Four others signed up at dinner, so they had to run heats.

By race time, there was a crowd of over one hundred waiting at the starting line, which was by the aft portside lifeboats.

Dave had lookouts placed strategically at each door. And Doris posted by the pool, a deck above, where she could watch over most of the course.

The first heat featured Bruce against a car dealer from Portland, Maine.

Before they started, Dave inspected each wheelchair.

The car dealer rubbed his arms with BENGAY and Bruce popped a digitalis. And they were off. Twice around the deck. As he crossed the finish line in first place, Bruce raised his hands over his head.

"WHOOPEE!" he said.

The final pitted Bruce Towler against Robert James, the real estate agent from Boca Raton.

Before they got it started, Bruce's daughter, Kathy, got wind of the race and came hustling up with Derek, the two of them determined to stop it. Doris spotted them, and they were intercepted and diverted into the dining room. They had to watch through the portside windows, Derek beet red, perspiring and pounding on the glass.

It was like the chariot race in *Ben Hur*—the two wheelchairs smashing against each other as they looped out of sight around the first-class cabins.

They were gone for less than a minute, but when they reappeared there was only one chair. Bruce Towler was nowhere to be seen.

"THE BUGGER STUCK HIS CANE IN MY SPOKES," said Bruce when he crossed the finish line a good two minutes later.

It was ten o'clock when the *Empress of Kumar* pulled back into Port Everglades. Dave and Morley were both on the upper deck as the ship eased through the seawall. Morley was leaning against the rail, looking back to sea. She was wearing a knee-length cream-silk dress covered with big green and white calla lilies. She was holding a glass of champagne.

"What are you thinking?" said Dave.

"Same thing I always think at the end of a trip," said Morley, turning to smile at him. "Glad to be home. Sad that it's over."

The ship blew its horn. She jumped a little.

"Scared me," she said. They were spending the last night in port. They were scheduled to get off in the morning.

On their way to their cabin, Dave and Morley passed Doris Schick and Bruce Towler. Doris was wearing a silver evening gown with a thousand silver sequins. Bruce Towler, sitting in his wheelchair, was clutching her silver sequined purse.

The letter came six months later.

It was from Bruce Towler's daughter, Kathy. Handwritten.

I am having a hard time with this.

My father would tell me to get off the pot. I should do that. He died last week.

That's the first time I have written that. It is so odd to see it written down.

Dave was reading the letter in his record store, leaning against the counter with the letter in front of him. He was alone, except for a guy he didn't know who was flipping through the blues section.

Dave looked up at the guy, and then he picked up the letter and counted the pages. He stared at them without reading for a moment. He was thinking of Bruce Towler. The afternoon of his big jump. Bruce hadn't even hesitated, not for a second.

Dave glanced back at the letter.

As these things go, it wasn't horrible. He drifted off watching *Extreme Wrestling*. He never woke up.

My father spoke of you often. He liked you a lot.

I don't know if you knew he was sick. I thought he was going to die on one of those cruises. He said you were the one who convinced him to move in with me.

He was always afraid of losing his independence. I always thought he would only come when he couldn't cope and he would feel defeated. He wasn't defeated at all. In fact, since that cruise he was happier, more energetic and more, I don't know, present, than he had been for years. He was a different person.

One night he even came to the movies with us. That might sound strange. You would have had to know him.

But of course you did.

Dave was nodding.

I was upset with you on the boat. I thought those things you did with him were—I feel so silly now—I thought they were dangerous.

He was so grateful for having met you. He said he never would have had the courage to leap if you hadn't been there that day. And I think he meant more than the jump.

I hope you don't mind me writing. I wanted you to know and I needed to thank you.

Here is my address. If you were ever this way, I would love you to drop by.

It was funny the things you set in motion without meaning to. It was like a big game of pool. You hit the balls and they start colliding and you never know where they are going to end up. All you do is take your best shot and stand back and watch them. And hope for the best.

It was a week later, a Sunday afternoon, just as Morley was leaving to pick up her mother for dinner, when Dave said, "Have you ever thought of asking her to live here, with us? I would be okay with that, if you did."

Morley was about to make a smart remark. And then she stopped, and saw he was serious. She came over to him, looked at him carefully and said, "Thank you."

It seemed to make her happy. She looked happy.

Dear Mr. McLean,

On a recent car trip, my husband was scanning the radio dial and came across your program, The Vinyl Cafe.

"Wow," said my husband, "that's still on the air?"

He says he figures you either have something on the president of CBC or you are the luckiest guy in show business.

Betting on the latter, I was wondering if you could pick my next round of lottery numbers?

With fingers crossed,
Angela

P.S. Just to be clear—if we win, we are not obligated to share our winnings with you or anything. Sorry.

Dear Angela,

Please find enclosed a series of my favourite numbers, ranging from one to one hundred. Take a close look at " thirty-six"; it's one I'm particularly fond of. I am also including a story about lottery tickets.

THE LOTTERY TICKET

There is no good time for bad news.

When something bad happens, people often say, "It couldn't have come at a worse time," but there *is* no better time when the news that comes is not the news you want. Bad news always has bad timing.

Stephanie's boyfriend, Tommy, hung up the phone and walked into his bathroom and stared into his bathroom mirror. He stood there for a long time. When he was finished staring, he went into his bedroom and picked up his grey hoodie off the floor. His toque was on top of the fridge. He fetched his toque, grabbed his notebook from the couch and headed out. Hands in his pockets. Shoulders hunched.

He didn't know it, but he was going to see Steph. He didn't go right there, though. He walked around for a good hour before he realized that's where he was heading.

Steph was in her kitchen when he arrived at her apartment. By the stove to be precise, holding a handful of pasta over a big pot. She was wearing an apron that said, *Procrastinate Now!* Tommy went to the back door, knocked on the window and walked in.

Stephanie was surprised to see him. He had said he was going to stay home and write.

She said, "What are you *doing* here?"

And, right out of the blue, just like he had appeared, just like the phone call, Tommy said, "My grandpa died."

Steph ran across the kitchen and gave him a hug. She said, "Are you okay?" Tommy dropped his canvas bag by the table. All Tommy said was, "I just don't believe it."

The first time Tommy took Stephanie to meet his grandpa was on his nineteenth birthday. A family dinner. It was a bit of a deal that he took her. He had never taken anyone before. Especially not a girl. She was nervous. She had talked way too much, but his grandpa liked her. He sat with her after dinner and talked about the war.

Tommy reached for Stephanie's hand. "He was at the barber's. He had ... a stroke. They didn't even take him to the hospital."

Ink.

That was what Tommy was thinking about.

Ink on his fingers. Ink on his shirt. His grandfather was plagued by ink. Now the old man had died and all Tommy could think about was what was going to happen to his grandpa's pens.

Stephanie said, "I was thinking about them too. Anyone would think that. That would come to anyone's mind."

Tommy's grandpa was ink stained.

He was the only person Stephanie knew who used a fountain pen. He had a collection of pens that he kept in a wooden box on his desk.

"This one is a Parker 51," he said holding up a sleek grey pen with a hooded nib.

"This is my Waterman." He took a glass bottle of ink out of the drawer and unscrewed it. Then he sniffed it.

"You have to be careful," he said, looking at her over his glasses. "Ink can go bad."

He took an eyedropper and used it to fill the Waterman. When he'd finished, there was a smudge of ink on his forehead. He handed Stephanie the pen. His initials were engraved on the gold clip. Then he got a piece of paper and laid it on the desk.

"You have to break a pen in," he said. "The paper wears the nib down for the way you write. It's a gold nib."

Stephanie looked at him. He nodded.

"Go on," he said.

She sat down and wrote her name.

"Imagine," he said. "Paper wearing down gold. You probably write with a safety pen."

"A ballpoint," said Stephanie.

"*Uh*," he said. "You might as well write with a nail."

He gave her one of his pens. It was a Waterman, tortoiseshell, with gold inlay. The first thing she wrote was a letter to him. Thank you. She sniffed the ink every time she filled the pen. She had no idea what bad ink smelled like.

Lewis J. Waterman was an insurance man. So was Tommy's grandfather. Waterman got drawn into the pen business after a leaky pen messed up one of his contracts. Tommy's grand-father, who was also Lewis, didn't go anywhere without *his* Waterman.

Tommy stayed at Stephanie's for dinner that night. It was while they were doing the dishes that Stephanie said, "Hey! What's going to happen to the ticket?"

Tommy said, "I hadn't thought about that."

His grandfather's famous lottery ticket. He had owned it for ten years.

"Longer," said Tommy. "Longer ... for sure. I remember it from when I was a kid."

There were different stories. Lewis bought the ticket after he had touched a bride. He bought it the day he found a four-leaf clover. He bought it with a hundred pennies that he had found, "heads up."

He had a whole routine with pennies he found. If they were "heads up," he kept them and made a wish. If they were "heads down," he would give them away—because "heads down" meant bad luck. So he had to give them away "heads up," to cancel the bad luck.

Tommy and Stephanie were sitting on her couch.

Tommy said, "When I was a kid, if I was with him when he found a penny, he would give *me* the wishes. Then he would make me tell him *what* I'd wished for. I told him you weren't supposed to tell. He said you were allowed to tell grandfathers."

Tommy stood up and started pacing. "I asked him about it when I was older."

Stephanie said, "I don't think he really believed it."

Tommy nodded.

Stephanie said, "Weird that he'd still do it, though."

Tommy said, "He told me he did it because he had heard that it still worked, even if you didn't believe."

So Tommy's grandfather had a lottery ticket. It was one of those scratch tickets from way back. There was no date on it, not even an expiry date. The prize was one million dollars.

That's what he used to say. "Imagine. A million dollars." Then he would say, "What would you do with a million dollars?" And you had to tell him what you would do.

Lewis would listen, ever so carefully. And when you were finished, he would say, "Are you sure that's what you would do? Is that your *heart's desire*?" And you had to go through the whole thing all over. It was all very serious because this, he told everyone, with absolute conviction, was a *winning* ticket. It might sound crazy, but he was a very convincing man.

The ticket was of considerable concern to the family. You might even say an obsession. It underlined shared points of view and it provoked differences. It got to be so everyone in the family, everyone, except perhaps the small children, had to have an opinion about the ticket. And when you settled on your stance, you had to defend it. Tommy's family argued about the ticket whenever they got together. They argued about it at family dinners. They argued about it at Christmas.

"Lewis!" shouted his brother. "A million dollars isn't what it used to be."

"It's still a million dollars," said Lewis.

"But if you had put it in the bank instead of leaving it on the mantel, you'd have collected interest. All these years. You know how much you would have?"

"Maybe I'd have nothing," Lewis would say. "Tommy, pass your mother the peas. You've read what happens to lottery winners. That man in Niagara Falls. That family in New Brunswick. I still have the million. How much does one man need?"

Then he would gesture toward the ticket, or maybe get up and walk over to the mantel where he kept it in a box. He might pick it up and wave it in the air.

Lewis believed having the dream was better than having the pile of money. Money? Well, money could cause no end of problems.

"It's far better to stick with dreams," he said.

Tommy said, "It used to drive my uncle nuts. My uncle thought he was crazy."

Stephanie pushed her hair away from her face and said, "What do you think?"

Tommy plopped onto the couch beside her and stretched out his legs. "I don't know," he said. "*He* was so sure. He was certain. I mean. It *could* be the winner. You can't deny that. It *could* be.

"Neighbours used to come to the house just to see it. Just to look at the winning ticket."

Steph said, "Do you think you should scratch it?"

Tommy said, "Do you think so?"

Steph said, "That way you'd know."

Tommy started to stand up and then sat down again.

"Because he is gone? Don't you think we should check the will?"

She hadn't thought of that. She hadn't thought of what he would want.

"He didn't mention it," said Tommy's father, holding his cellphone against his chest.

"Don't you think that's odd?" said Tommy's mother.

"What?" said Tommy's father. "That it wasn't mentioned? Or that I am phoning a lawyer to ask him to re-check my father's will to make certain that he didn't mention an unscratched lottery ticket that he had on his mantelpiece for over a decade. Yes. Now that you ask, I think it's odd."

"What would happen," said Stephanie, "if you scratched it, and it was a winner?"

"I would feel bad for not trusting him," said Tommy. "For not believing."

"And if it wasn't a winner?"

"I would just feel bad."

The funeral was scheduled for Monday. Tommy went home on Thursday. By the time he got there, the whole neighbourhood was buzzing. No one had a say, but everyone had an opinion.

Wherever Tommy went, they were talking about it. And they all wanted to tell him what they thought. They were talking about it at the funeral parlour.

"Tommy, the reason he didn't mention it in the will is

because he knew it wasn't a winner. He knew it was worthless. You should just scratch it and be done with it."

They were talking about it at the corner store.

"Ahmed, if you are so sure it is *not* a winning ticket, why are you in a such a hurry for the boy to scratch it? If you are so sure, you should tell him to throw it out."

And they were talking about it at the barbershop—the very place where Lewis had had his stroke.

"Tommy, I went to your grandpa's house once, so he could show it to me. I have a picture. In the picture I am holding the ticket."

"Maybe we could scratch the picture."

Some were believers. "It made him happy," they'd say. "And no harm was done. Everyone should have such a thing."

Others thought the whole thing was foolish.

"It is not the original ticket," claimed one. "He scratched the original ticket years ago. He won five bucks. That's all. I know a guy who was there when he did it. It was only five bucks. The guy told me."

The whole neighbourhood was divided into two camps, the scratchers and the non-scratchers. The believers and the ones who didn't believe.

The night before the funeral, Tommy's family gathered at Tommy's house. After dinner Tommy, Tommy's father and Tommy's great-uncle, Lawrence, were sitting at the dining-room table. The ticket was lying on the table.

Lewis used to torment Uncle Lawrence with the ticket. He would bring the ticket out at family dinners and lay it front of him and watch him squirm.

"Watch him squirm," he would say.

And oh, he would squirm. "Lewis," he would start, "it is arrogant to say that money doesn't matter."

"Arrogant?" Tommy's grandfather didn't have to say much. He would poke his brother Lawrence now and again if he was running out of steam. "Arrogant?"

"It is irresponsible. If *you* don't want the money, you should use it for something else. Send the grandchildren to university."

He said that at Christmas this year. And when he did, Lewis twinkled. He winked at Tommy and said, "But the grandchildren are *already* at university."

Uncle Lawrence said, "Bah! Give it to charity then."

And that's when Lewis pounced. Lewis said, "Ah ... now we're talking. Tell me exactly which charity. Come on. What would you do if you had *a million dollars?*"

Uncle Lawrence knew he had been suckered again, and he slapped the table. And that was the end of that.

"It's not about the money," said Uncle Lawrence, for the third or fourth time. "I don't want the money—it's the principle."

"If it's not about the money," said Tommy's father, "then what's the hurry? How many years have we have gone without scratching? We can't wait until he's buried?"

And so it was decided. They would wait until after the funeral. And after the funeral, when everyone was together, they would scratch the ticket.

Even though the family had made their decision, the debate echoed in their minds. So although everyone agreed that the Rev. Simms spoke nicely at the service, it was hard not to think that he had weighed in on the subject.

"Lewis was a man of faith," said the Reverend in his homily. "And faith is the ability to believe in something that cannot be proven."

"What is he talking about?" said Uncle Lawrence under his breath. "We scratch it and we know. It's as simple as that. There's the proof."

"Be quiet," whispered Lawrence's wife. "He isn't talking about the ticket. Show some respect for your dead brother."

"Hocus-pocus," muttered Uncle Lawrence.

Back at the house after the service, there was a lot of discussion about what the Reverend Simms had meant.

"What he is saying," said Tommy's father, "is if you *believe* you know, then you know. That's what faith is."

Tommy's head was spinning. If you were among the faithful, then, you believed that scratching the ticket would be a loss of faith. Lewis had had faith. He hadn't needed to scratch the ticket.

Uncle Lawrence was sitting in Lewis's favourite chair. He had a coffee cup perched precariously on the arm.

"Lawrence," said Tommy's father, "owning that ticket gave him hope. Maybe he needed hope more than he needed money."

"Hope," said Uncle Lawrence, "is false and foolish. All he had was *false* hope."

"*Hope*," said Tommy's father, "keeps despair at bay."

"Not mine," said Uncle Lawrence. "I despair that I'm living in a family of idiots."

There were seven people around the table on Tuesday night: Tommy, Tommy's mother, Tommy's father, Uncle Lawrence, Lawrence's wife, Muriel, his aunt Edith and Edith's son, Tony.

Tony was the youngest. When everyone was settled, Uncle Lawrence nodded at Tony and Tony got up from the dining-room table and walked to the mantel. He carried the wooden box carefully across the room and placed it in front of Uncle Lawrence, who was the oldest. Tommy was sitting opposite Uncle Lawrence. Tommy squeezed his eyes closed as Uncle Lawrence opened the box.

Uncle Lawrence looked into the box and then slowly around the table. Then he picked the box up and held it so everyone could see in. Lewis's faded lottery ticket was gone. There were seven brand-new tickets in its place.

And so a week passed.

And Tommy and Stephanie were back at her apartment.

Tommy said, "It was only a week ago."

Tommy was sitting at the table where he had sat that night. He was holding a beer.

Stephanie said, "I wish I could have been there when you told them."

Tommy said, "My father laughed. No one else said *anything*. What could they say? I put the ticket in Grandpa's pocket. The ticket was *buried*. They weren't going to dig him up."

Tommy stumbled over the word *buried*. He started to cry.

"Whoa," he said. "That took a while."

"It is okay," said Stephanie. "It's about time."

She waited. Then she said, "I wish I could have seen your uncle Lawrence. I wish you had a video."

"Yeah," said Tommy. "He surprised me. I thought he would have scratched *his* right away. To make a point. But no one did."

Then she said, "Why did you do it?"

"Because," said Tommy. "I trusted him."

Stephanie said, "I think he would have liked you to have it."

Tommy said, "The money?"

Stephanie said, "Not the money. The dream."

And Tommy said, "I do." And he reached into his pocket, and he pulled out *his* ticket.

"I bought seven," he said.

Stephanie held out her hand, and he handed it to her.

Stephanie said, "Do you think it's a winner?"

And Tommy said, "Oh I *know* it is. I am *sure* it's a winner. You can tell."

Stephanie said, "Are we going to scratch it?"

Tommy said, "No. We're going to hold onto it. Just in case."

Stephanie said, "Just in case what? We need the money?"

Tommy said, "No. We don't need the money. We'll never need money. In case we need him."

"But Grandpa," said Tommy.

This is a long time ago. He is remembering this part from a long time ago. To be honest he is not even sure this part happened. When he remembers it, it seems like a dream to him. Maybe he had imagined it. But this is the way he remembers it.

"But Grandpa," he says, "it's just a dream of a dream."

And his grandfather says, "Now you've got it. Now you understand. It's just a dream. That is exactly what it is. It is nothing at all. And in the dream, I am still here. I am still with you. I may seem to be gone, but I have only gone on a little trip. Whatever I was once, I am still. When you see a penny, you must pick it up for me. Save all the ones that are 'heads up' in the little jar the way we do.

"And tonight, when you are falling asleep, I want you to think very hard, because tomorrow, when you wake up, I want you to tell me exactly what you would do if you had *a million dollars*. I want you to tell me your heart's desire."

Dear Stuart,

For as long as I can remember, I've been plagued by a vast assortment of irrational fears. You seem like a guy with more than a few irrational fears of your own, so I thought you might have a few suggestions about a recent dilemma in which I find myself. My new girlfriend is wild about rides and has said that as soon as the local amusement park opens in the spring, she wants me to take her on the new roller coaster. Now, I suffer from a fear of (1) amusement parks, (2) heights, (3) roller coasters and (4) commitment. Do you have any advice for me?

In anxious anticipation of your response,
Howard

Dear Howard,

Please see below.

DAVE AND THE ROLLER COASTER

The town of Big Narrows, in Cape Breton, Nova Scotia, the town where Dave grew up, was, when Dave was a boy, about as far away as you could get from anywhere.

Not that there weren't plenty of places in town to keep a boy happy. There was the alley full of steam that ran alongside Art Gillespie's Laundromat. Down by the river there was the chair factory, and you could always find scrap wood there. If you were lucky enough to have a little money, there was MacDonnell's Post Office and General Store, which is where kids went for candy, pop and *Mad Magazine*; teens went for smokes; and parents picked up the big-city papers: *The Glace Bay Coastal Courier*, *The Antigonish Casket*.

Big Narrows was off the main road, no doubt about it. Still is. When Dave was a boy, he knew the summer slowness of dirt roads, and spent hours at the trouting pond on Macaulay's mountain. Or at the jumping cliff in the hills.

It was Dave's cousin Brenda who discovered the jumping cliff. Brenda who discovered you could leap off the cliff, and then, as you flew through the air, save yourself from smashing to the ground by grabbing onto the high branches of one of the maple saplings that grew at the cliff base. The saplings would bend gracefully and lower you to the ground. It was like pole-vaulting in reverse. On a Saturday afternoon in May, you could go up the hill, and there would be kids flying through the forest like monkeys.

The kids were always up to something in the Narrows. The summer Dave was eleven, Billy Mitchell found an old grey and green Verchères rowboat at the dump. The next morning, he assembled nine boys. It took them all morning, and half the afternoon, but they lugged the boat, all leaky and rotten and done in, down the dam road. They got it to the pond in one piece, and they played pirates for the rest of that summer, dividing into teams—the English rowing the doomed boat along the shore, the French pirates swamping out from under the pine trees that hung low over the water, the boys' yelps echoing over the hills for hours.

At night they would meet, the boys and the girls, in big packs of sparking energy, and they played hide-and-seek, and kick the can; and when they got tired of that, if it wasn't time for them to go home, they drifted off to the schoolyard, where they took turns on the swings, arching back and forth under the cover of darkness, under skies as clear and starry as any sky anywhere.

It was, all in all, just about a perfect place to grow up, although you'd never convince any of the kids of that. When you do your growing up in a place like the Narrows, where you know everything about everyone, and everyone *thinks* they know everything about you, you spend a lot of time dreaming of the places you are going to go the day you can finally swing clear of the schoolyard and over the moon.

Dave dreamt of landing in Brooklyn, New York, home of the

most famous amusement park in the world, Coney Island. When he got there, he was going to ride the roller coaster. The world-famous Cyclone. He had read, in the *Reader's Digest*, that it was the fastest roller coaster in the world—so fast it defied gravity. Billy Mitchell said the Mercury astronauts used to go to Coney Island and train at night.

Billy and Dave had a plan to go the summer they were fifteen. They never made it, of course, and soon enough life took over. To everything there is a season. Dave *missed* the season of roller coasters.

And he'd forgotten about them for twenty long years, until the leafy summer his son, Sam, was six. It all came back on a summer afternoon, sitting in a schoolyard, watching Sam, as he pumped back and forth on a swing.

Dave wasn't thinking about roller coasters. Dave wasn't thinking about anything, really. He was just sitting there the way you do, enjoying Sam on the swing, enjoying, especially, the moment at the high point of each forward arc, when his son was virtually upside down, his legs kicking at the sky, his head falling back—that motionless moment before gravity asserted itself, and the cables on the swing buckled, and the inevitable return to earth.

Dave was lost in the peaceful pumping of his pendulum son, until Sam abruptly ended the moment by launching himself off the swing. He left it at the strategically perfect moment, using the centrifugal force to catapult himself into the air, *alarmingly* high and fast, his little arms and legs flapping as he tried to keep himself upright. A little cannonball.

Dave gasped and lurched off the bench. He began to run across the park toward his son, in horror.

Well, part of Dave was running toward Sam in horror. Another part of Dave was still sitting on the bench thinking, *Wow, that looks like fun.*

Then Sam hit the ground, with a thump and roll, a twist of arms and legs. *That* didn't look like fun. And then there was a moment of profound silence.

And in that moment, the part of Dave that he had left behind on the bench sighed and got up and started loping across the field too, thinking as it did, *I wonder if he was actually weightless.*

Sam sat up, holding his arm.

"I'm okay," he said. "I'll be fine."

Which is exactly what the emergency-room doctor said as he put on the cast.

"You'll be fine," said the doctor. "We'll see you in six weeks."

Dave took Sam to the amusement park before the cast came off, which would have been fine, or should have been, except Sam was only six, way too young. And Dave, who was old enough to know better, was way too keen.

But the seed had been replanted, and when they got there, the first thing they did was to get in line for the roller coaster.

As the line moved closer, close enough for Sam to see what they were waiting for, he began to whimper.

Dave said, "Come on, it will be fun."

Sam shook his head.

Dave picked Sam up, more or less lovingly, and held him close. He began whispering calming, reassuring things. Sam seemed to relax a little. Dave continued his supplication.

"Look," said Dave, pointing at the roller coaster.

The people sitting in the roller coaster looked terrified. They were clinging to one another. A woman in the front was screaming. Sam couldn't imagine what horrible thing was happening to them, but he knew from the way the lady was screaming it was bad. He didn't want any part of it.

"It'll be fun," Dave said. "It's just like riding on a swing."

At the word *swing* Sam stiffened and began to squirm in Dave's arms.

"No, no, no, no, no," said Sam. Then he collapsed into tears.

Dave's shoulders sagged. It was time to concede defeat. He turned and began to work his way back down the line, "Excuse me, I'm sorry. Excuse me please." Sam was crying and thrashing, the cast flailing around like a club.

They finally made it to the entrance, where Dave spotted a weary-looking father being dragged to the roller coaster by three loud and highly enthusiastic children. As this small group pushed past them, Sam's swinging plaster-encased arm clipped the defeated father full on the nose. Dave heard a crunch. The man staggered under the blow. His hands flew up to his nose.

"I'm bleeding," cried the man.

Dave didn't even look over his shoulder. Dave kept going.

Dave and Sam spent the rest of the afternoon hiding out in Kiddieland—a quiet and grassy oasis, with a climber, a cage of coloured vinyl balls and a slide in the shape of an elephant. Sam played happily, while Dave sat morosely on a bench pulling little bits of cotton candy out of the hairs on his legs.

They went back the summer Sam was eight. This time they were better prepared. They talked about roller coasters for weeks before they went. Sam was pumped. They lined up for forty sticky minutes. When they got to the front of the line, a man wearing a duck costume took one look at Sam, shook his head and said, "Not tall enough."

"What?" said Dave.

"Fifty-four inches," said the man. "He's too short."

People began to push past them. They headed back to Kiddieland. Sam pointed at a ride. A circle of giant bumblebees that went around and around in a small slow circle. Dave and Sam watched it for ten minutes, standing right beside the fence so it appeared as if the bumblebees were flying right at them.

Sam said, "Can I try it?"

He rode the bumblebees three times. After his third turn, he staggered off and said, "I don't feel too good." Then he threw up.

Then, one night two summers later, Sam said, "I still haven't been on a roller coaster."

They went back to the park again. Just the two of them.

They went late on a Friday afternoon. Sam rode his bike to the record store. When he got there, Dave and Brian were playing a game of Ringo. A house favourite. They use a homemade launcher to shoot plastic forty-five record centres at a turntable, trying to land them on the spindle.

"Hey," said Sam, as he walked in.

"Hey," said Dave, firing a record centre at his son. "I'm pumped. You pumped?"

They got falafel from a little family-run falafel place and ate in the car. They arrived at the park at 6:30. The sun was beginning to dip. It was the perfect time—to be coming as the day was going. They bought a roll of tickets.

The park was full. *Just as it should be*, thought Dave. You wouldn't want the place to yourself. Diving into the crowd was like shoving a canoe into a stretch of whitewater. The river of people picked you up and carried you along. Somewhere, mixed with the noise of the crowd and the ringing bells, floating above the red and yellow flashing lights, Dave could hear Cream singing "Sunshine of Your Love" through a tinny PA system.

They walked passed Kiddieland.

"Remember?" said Dave, pointing.

Sam shook his head. "No, what?"

"Nothing," said Dave.

It took them twenty minutes to get to the roller coaster.

A lot has happened in the world of roller-coaster design over the last forty years.

Dave had missed all of it.

They were standing in front of The Hypergeist—a roller coaster that the sign said would exert a force of 4.2 Gs as it tossed and flipped its way through two loops and a corkscrew.

Slouched against a control panel was a young guy with long hair tied in a ponytail and a ring through his eyebrow. He was wearing a Black Sabbath T-shirt and torn black jeans. He looked bored and inattentive as he waved people onto the ride. Hardly the kind of person you want with their hands on the controls of a two-ton steel machine meant to convey hundreds of innocent people around a raised track at break-neck speeds.

"Has anyone ever had an accident on this ride?" said Dave as he looked for the tickets.

"Not that I've ever noticed," said the guy.

An older fellow in overalls wandered over and said it was time for the young guy's break.

The older guy looked more on the ball.

Dave said, "Exactly how fast does it go?"

"Depends on the weather," said the guy in the coveralls.

"The weather?" said Dave, clearly unnerved.

The man shrugged. "The wind slows it down." He nodded at the sky. "Night like this, hot like this, it goes a lot faster. Or when the rails get wet. Hard to stop it when the rails are wet."

The idea of variables made Dave edgy. He had assumed there were no variables. He had assumed that his ride would be like all the other rides. The ones that had come back safely.

Sam said, "Let's get in line."

There was a big sign just before the platform. Dave grabbed Sam by the shoulder and restrained him. He said, "Just a minute." Dave wanted to read the sign.

Do not speak to operator.

Do not walk on the track.

Do not put arms outside the car.

Do not ride if pregnant.

Do not ride if you suffer from heart palpitations, vertigo, high blood pressure, atrial fibrillation, night sweats, anxiety disorder or peanut allergy.

"Come on," said Sam.

Dave said, "Just a minute." Dave kept reading.

This ride may cause shortness of breath, excessive sweating and dry mouth.

Dave mopped his brow on the sleeve of his shirt. He was having a hard time catching his breath; his tongue was sticking to the roof of his mouth.

Some people may experience nausea, confusion, disorientation, muscle twitches or an overwhelming desire to urinate.

Dave crossed his legs and began bobbing up and down slowly. He squinted at the sign.

Do not go on this ride if you have silver amalgam fillings, or worry about going mad, or have had precognitive experiences that involve hurtling to your death in an amusement park while trapped in a grisly little car that leaves the rails and you didn't have to go if you didn't want to and that will be your last thought.

"Huh?" said Dave.

"Come *on*," said Sam.

"I'm not sure I can do this," said Dave.

"Oh brother," said Sam.

For the second time in their lives, they slunk out of line. As they passed a group of teenagers, Sam muttered, "They won't let him on the ride. He's pregnant."

"What is the problem?" said Sam.

"I *can't* do this," said Dave.

They were sitting on a park bench. They were eating cotton candy. They were passing a pop back and forth.

Sam said, "It's normal to be afraid. You are supposed to be afraid. You aren't going to die. You can't die."

Dave thought, *Sometimes people die.*

Sam said, "Not here. Not tonight. That would be ridiculous. What are you afraid of?"

They finished their candy. They finished their pop.

Dave said, "I don't know *what* I'm afraid of. I'm just afraid."

Sam stood up and held out his hand.

Dave said, "Go without me. I'll watch."

Sam said, "I have a better idea."

"Okay," said Dave.

Sam said, "Do you trust me?"

What could he say to that? He nodded his head.

Sam said, "Good. Okay. Stand up and close your eyes. Promise me you won't open them until I tell you."

Dave closed his eyes. Sam took his father's hand.

Dave said, "If I die I am going to *keeel* you."

Sam said, "Just don't open your eyes."

Sam led him through the park; through the bumps and the bells, and the screams, and Dave didn't open his eyes. Not once. It was very, very hard. But Dave kept his eyes closed.

And then they stopped. Sam let go of his father's hand and walked up to a park carney. He said: "My father needs help. He's blind."

Dave *really* wanted to open his eyes now, but now he

couldn't. Now he *had* to keep them closed because the man had him by the elbow and was helping him into a seat.

As he sat down, Dave put out his hand and felt the seat. And *ohmigod* he wanted to peek so badly, but the man was right there. Dave could feel his breath, could sense him, reaching across. He was fastening Dave's seat belt. He could sense Sam sitting beside him. He could sense the car starting to move.

Sam said, "Are you scared?"

Dave said, "Yes. I'm scared. But it's okay."

Sam said, "Don't be afraid."

They were moving slowly.

"This isn't so bad," said Dave.

"It's going to be okay," said Sam.

Dave said, "Can I open my eyes?"

Sam said, "Not yet."

They were picking up speed.

"I can feel it," said Dave.

And then Sam said, "Okay. Now!"

And Dave, who had been clutching the bar in front of him, didn't open his eyes right away. Instead he lifted his hands off the bar, and he held his arms in the air over his head just like they did in the pictures you see of people on roller coasters and he yelled like those people. He yelled as loud as he could. "AAAAYYYIEEEEEE."

Then he opened his eyes. And saw he was on the giant bumblebee ride. Sam was sitting beside him with his head in his hands. And a group of adults, whom he had never seen before in his life, were waving as he circled slowly past them.

Dave said, "What are we doing?"

Sam said, "De-conditioning you."

They went into the Giggle Palace, and stood in front of the funhouse mirrors. Sam's mirror stretched him tall and impossibly thin. Dave's made him look like an overweight child.

Perfect, thought Dave. He couldn't say when it had happened but he wasn't going to deny it. He couldn't keep up with his children anymore. His son knew more about computers and iPods than he ever would. His daughter had just sent him an email about a music group he had never heard of. He felt as if he had to run just to keep up these days, and even though he was running as fast as he could, he knew he was slipping behind. His children were passing him on the highway of life. *This* was just another milestone along the way. Soon there would be plenty more. And that wasn't the worst part. One day, before he knew it, he would have to pull over and wave goodbye. Sam would leave him behind.

"Okay," said Dave. "Let's do it."

"Are you sure?" said Sam

"No," said Dave. "But let's do it anyway."

And so off they headed across the park for the second time. Back to the lineup they had quit three times now. As they came abreast of the warning sign, Dave said, "I'm just going to shut my eyes for a moment." And that's what he did. Sam led him along the line, talking all the time. "When we get there, look ahead at the track in front of you. It will make you feel balanced. When we start up, keep your body relaxed, and let your neck and shoulders go limp. If you start to feel queasy, push your right foot down into the floor, grab the bar like a steering wheel and pretend you are driving it."

Dave opened his eyes and stared at Sam.

"How do you know this stuff?'

Sam said, "I got it off the net."

Dave said, "You researched this?"

Sam shrugged. "I figured you might need some help."

Before Dave knew it, they were climbing into a little car. Sam turned and looked at his father earnestly, "Remember," he said, "you only have to do this once."

Dave said, "Is that from the net too?"

Sam nodded. "You can repeat it to yourself if it helps."

A heavy, padded bar fell across Dave's lap. He felt a rush of panic. He didn't have a choice anymore. *I only have to do this once.* He looked at Sam and grinned. Sam gave him the thumbs-up. Suddenly there was a noise like rocket fuel burning, and Dave's stomach tightened, and they exploded out of the station. Zero to eighty in two seconds. An abrupt left-hand turn, and Sam was leaning into him. Then a turn to the right. That wasn't so bad. And they seemed to be slowing. Dave glanced at Sam. Was it over?

Sam shook his head and pointed. The track was rising in front of them. They were climbing a huge hill. Tilting backwards. Slower and slower. Way back. Dave nodded. Closed his eyes. *I only have to do this once.* Then they crested the top and were plunging to the ground, and Dave could feel himself coming right out of his seat. He was airborne. And *ohmigod* the cars ahead of him were flipping over. He was airborne. He was upside down. He was right side up. He was coming. He was going. Someone was screaming. Someone was screaming from the pit of their bowels. Something terrible had happened to someone nearby. Dave opened his eyes and turned to his right and checked Sam.

Sam's hair was blowing in the wind. He looked like Arthur their dog when he stuck his head out the car window.

They were flying though the air. The screams sounded horrible. Someone was being dragged or something. He opened his mouth to ask Sam if he was okay—and realized his mouth was already open, realized that *he* was the guy screaming. It had begun as a scream of terror. But it was different now, it wasn't a scream of terror anymore, it was a scream of unadulterated joy. Sam was screaming too. The two of them screaming like fools.

Sam lifted his hands and held them over his head. He motioned to Dave to do the same.

Dave was clutching the padded bar, his foot pushed into the floor.

"I can't," he screamed. "I'm driving."

And then it was over.

Just like that.

Just like that—around a corner and they pulled in to the station.

And Sam held his hand up and Dave uncurled his fingers from the bar one by one and high-fived his son. He said, "I've never done that before."

And Sam said, "How do you feel?"

And Dave said, "I feel like a kid.

Then he said, "Again?"

On their way out of the park, they walked by a merry-go-round—a beautifully restored carousel of the old style. Painted wooden ponies with genuine leather reins.

Dave held up the last of their tickets. "Come on," he said.

"No way," said Sam.

So Dave went alone. It was late. He was the only person on the ride. He chose a big white horse, frozen on its brass pole, its wild mouth tossing backwards.

As the ride began, Dave looked at all the empty horses in front and beside him, all the horses going up and down, up and down, the calliope, and the horses going up and down, and the carousel spinning around. It was like the gallop of life—it was like his life—galloping all alone to a place that was out there somewhere, but kept fading into the distance the closer he got.

Around and around he went. Each time he passed Sam, he lifted his hand and waved. And that was when he realized he had been wrong at the hall of mirrors. Well, partly wrong. He *was* falling behind—he'd got that part right.

But Sam wasn't going to leave him on the sidelines. His son was hurtling into the future, no doubt about it, but Dave wasn't being left behind. He was being dragged along with him. This *was* the future, this moment and all the others. It was the same old thing. The way it had been ever since Sam was born. His son was opening him to life. His son had taught *him* more than *he* would ever teach his son.

Around and around. Sam was leaning on the fence watching. Dave waved like a kid. Sam shook his head, ruefully.

And then he disappeared from view again, as the carousel carried Dave out of sight, smiling as he rode his silly wooden horse. Waving. Above all happy.